OTHER LIKELY STORIES

Debra Leigh Scott

OTHER LIKELY STORIES

SOWILO PRESS
Philadelphia   2010

Library of Congress Control Number: 2010930191

ISBN 978-0-9844727-1-0

 SOWILO PRESS
An imprint of Hidden River Publishing
P.O. Box 421
Bala Cynwyd, PA 19004, USA

CONTENTS

INTRODUCTION

I don't think I work like most writers. First of all, it takes me years and years to finish something—even a short story. It also took me years of being frustrated with myself before I realized that the reason for this slow process was that each story I write is only one sliver of a world I am continually discovering.

These short stories will introduce you to characters I have lived with now for a very long time. Two of the characters here, Rachael and Midgy Meade, are sisters, growing up at Fort Bragg during one of the most tumultuous times in our country's history—the era of the Vietnam War, in the social and political ruptures of the sixties. Their cousin, Marlena Galloway, is also a main character in these stories. Her story intertwines with theirs but includes a struggle with the racial issues of those same years. I think of these stories as sketches, not because they aren't complete stories, but because they are glimpses into, and investigations of, a larger world. That world is a place I move more deeply into in the trilogy of novels I have also spent a decade of my life writing. If you read the novels, you will recognize the characters you meet here, but storylines and situations within the novels may not be the same. They might be experienced from a different character's perspective, or they might turn out differently. These stories, in some cases, reveal things about the characters that you won't know by reading the novels. I think of the stories as studies in contradictions. Like the studies made by a visual artist for a larger work, these stories examine, in close up, some of the elements of the larger work, and peer into the lives of these three characters specifically. The stories span the period of time from 1955 to 1975. In the table of contents, I've included notes as to which character's story each one is, and in what year the story takes place.

ACKNOWLEDGMENTS

THE STORIES IN THIS BOOK have appeared in slightly different form in the following literary magazines: "All the Accidents of Man" as "The Accidents of Man" in *The Oxford American* and "All the Accidents of Man" in *The Abiko Quarterly*, "A Kind of Heaven" in *The Chattahoochee Review*, "Red" in *Miranda*, "Memorial Day" in *TPQ*, "What We Love" in *Words of Wisdom*, "A Fire Goeth Before Him" in *The Ashen Eye*, "Some of the T-Bone Stories" in *River City*. I'd like to thank the editors and say how much these journals offer to the literary community. You are crucial to publishing, even more now than ever before. Thanks for the incredible dedication and bravery you show in your continuing support of literature and writing in an age showing so little appreciation for the arts.

These stories were written over a long period of time—well over ten years, in fact. During those years, I have been grateful for the guidance, encouragement and support of many. I'd like to attempt to thank them here, and state publicly how much they have meant to me.

The earliest group of people to whom I owe gratitude is the Rittenhouse Writers' Group in Philadelphia, and to its founder, James Rahn. They were the first readers of my earliest stories, and provided an enormous amount of encouragement and advice to a writer who was still having a hard time calling herself one. Richard Burgin, Editor of *Boulevard*, and a friend, offered advice and support in those earliest years as well. The Temple University Creative Writing Program also provided support and guidance. I'd like to especially thank Joan Mellen, for her ongoing, unflagging encouragement and advice. I would also like to express gratitude to the wonderful, late, Bill Van Wert, who often saw what I was trying to do, long before I did. Two fellow students in the program continued to provide critique and encouragement years after we finished our degree; they are Virginia Nalencz and Clare Coleman. Thanks to you both. I'd like to thank Lewis Nordan for his kindness and his advice. The most ongoing, amazing, heart-warming support has come from fellow members of the Working Writers Group. I could never have written these stories, or anything else I've worked on, or am working on, without the combination of brilliant minds and dedicated hearts that exist in this group! My thanks, with much love, goes to Ann de Forest, Doug Gordon, Louis Greenstein, Larry Loebell, Mark Lyons, Ligia Ravé, David Sanders, and Miriam Seidel.

Several organizations have provided financial support and professional guidance, as well. I would like to acknowledge The Pennsylvania Council of the Arts, which awarded me artist's grants for several of my short stories in this collection. The Leeway Foundation provided some financial support. The Pirate's Alley Faulkner Society in New Orleans recognized several of these short stories as finalists in their yearly competition. The Sewanee Writers' Conference named me Tennessee Williams Scholar and provided me with the wonderful experience of working with fellow writers for a wonderful time in the Tennessee mountains. Thanks especially to Cheri Peters, Wyatt Prunty, and to my mentors at the conference, Amy Hempel and the late Barry Hannah. I'd like to make special mention here of Elwood Reid, a fellow writer, and attendee at Sewanee that summer, who gave me the best piece of advice I have ever gotten about my writing. "You've got your hands on the shoulders of this character and you're pushing her through the story," he said. "Let go, get the hell out of the way, and let her do what she needs to do." Thanks, Elwood. You were right.

My gratitude goes, too, to the Writing Aloud Program of the InterAct Theatre, and to its Founder, David Sanders. Two of these short stories, "Some of the T-Bone Stories" and "What We Love," were honored by being chosen for the program, and were read aloud by professional actors.

Thanks to Katie Baker and Alice George, students of Rosemont College's Master's Program in Publishing, and to their teacher, Carla Spataro, of *Philadelphia Stories*, who pored over these pages, editing and correcting, and who have provided the one thing every writer needs: a marketing plan.

Finally, and most especially, thanks and love go to my wonderful children, Maria Lisa and Daniel Joshua. Thanks for your love, your encouragement, and for being two of the most amazing human beings ever to walk the earth! I will never know why I was blessed with the gift of being your parent, but I will always be grateful for it.

OTHER LIKELY STORIES

For Maria Lisa and Daniel Joshua

> *. . . Ah, the dreamers ride against the men of action,*
> *Oh, see the men of action falling back . . .*
> — *Leonard Cohen*

Leaving Piety

"HUSH NOW. STAY SMALL," Tessa hissed, "or they'll see you in a lightning flash and come possess your soul."

In the onyx walls of water pouring down through the sky, Tessa swore there were arms and legs torn from bodies unseen floating in the air, figures terrible to behold rising big as trees, flying through the winds. When the rain beat hard against the flatroof balcony, the lashing drops bounced again and again, hammering.

"Hear them?" Tessa whimpered. "That's spirits, banging to be let in."

"I *never* see these ghosts." The child's cool voice came from the dark.

"Well, you surely will," Tessa whispered. "Once your purity's finally gone."

Through deep shadow, Rachael saw the outline of her great-aunt's body curled fearfully on the dressing room floor beneath garment bags of dresses, chinchilla and minks. The child knew she would have no choice but to sleep with Tessa beneath the racks of clothing in the total darkness of the closet until the storm had passed.

In sunlight the following day, Tessa was calm again, acting as if she never had any fears or demons, painting up her face with expensive bottles and jars spread out across the makeup table.

Rachael sat on the rug at her great-aunt's feet, marking a coloring book fiercely, going out of the lines.

"Will your ghosts hurt me, Aunt Tessa?" she asked.

Tessa lowered the mascara brush and turned toward the five-year-old.

"When have I ever let anything hurt you?" she asked.

"Never," Rachael said.

"Who always takes care of you?"

"You do," Rachael answered.

Tessa smiled. "Whoever loves you better than me?"

"Never *mind*," Rachael said, returning to her crayons. She pulled a color from the box and streaked it hard across the page of her coloring book, a slash of deep crimson.

It was New Orleans, 1955. Outside their door in the French Quarter, ghosts walked unseen among the living. Down secret streets, behind hidden doors, candles flickered, incantations drew spirits into flesh, pulled souls from their bodies. People in New Orleans believed. Rituals, Holy Days, talismans, blood gifts, *gris gris* bags—all practices to protect the living from creatures of a darker world. But sometimes, it is said, the wrong ones got protected. And sometimes it seemed protection didn't come at all.

"Your turn," Tessa said.

The child came forward and Tessa took her upturned chin, applying colors, guiding Rachael's small fingers to smudge the lipstick and pat the sky-blue eye shadow above her chocolate eyes.

"You are the most beautiful child," Tessa said. Then dropping her voice, although no one else was there to hear, she held the child to her breast. "God help me," she whispered, "but you are my favorite."

Rachael wriggled free. "I think it's a school day."

Tessa laughed. "What's so all-fired important about a school day, honey? Did I forget to say? I talked to your mama last night."

"When?" Rachael asked.

Tessa rarely answered the telephone when it rang. And once last night she walked toward the ringing and lifted the receiver, dropping it back on the cradle, silent again.

"You don't want to leave me, do you?" Tessa frowned. She ran a comb through Rachael's sable-colored hair.

Rachael's teacher at George Washington Elementary had promised more picture books about Greek gods, and she was anxious to bring them home. She wanted to find a picture of Icarus, in his chariot.

"How come mommy didn't talk to me?" she asked.

"Didn't want to, honey. Hold still." Tessa attempted to fasten a barrette into place. "She said for you to stay a few more days. She said of *course* we should go shopping."

Rachael stared at her great-aunt, not believing. At first, the child had liked being at Tessa's home better than the one she and her mother shared on Piety Street. It had enormous rooms, with a wide and sunny front porch where she liked to sit on a rocking chair and look at picture books of places far away. There was a pretty Creole lady named Tildie DuValle who came each day and cleaned until everything sparkled like new. Tildie cooked them gumbo and étouffée, and folded the fresh-smelling laundry into dresser drawers. Everything on Esplanade appeared to be just right. But for Rachael, it had all become the kind of fairy tale where nothing was as it seemed. Sometimes Rachael spied on Tildie, who waved her hands over the bubbling gumbo when she thought she was alone, whispering magic words and sprinkling crushed eggshell into the steaming brew. Hiding behind the planted palms on the upstairs porch, Rachael sometimes watched Tildie kneel behind a tangle of red roses in the courtyard below, leaving apples and plantains at the feet of a little brown figure, a man with a great hammer raised in the air. Tessa was growing more and more nervous with each storm that came through the Delta, and she refused to open the big beautiful windows anymore, leaving them shuttered against the light of the outside world.

An olive-skinned man whose framed photographs were set on tables and dressers around the rooms Tessa said was Uncle Biagio. His face seemed frightening and Rachael was glad she never saw him in all the times she was there.

"He's in Havana," Tessa told her once.

To Rachael, the word sounded like "banana" and she decided that Tessa made it up, that maybe Biagio was the spirit her great-aunt was afraid of, the one who appeared in the thunderstorms and made the beating sounds that caused her to cower and cry.

"I don't want to go shopping," Rachael said.

"Don't be silly," Tessa said. "Of course you do. Nobody wants to be poor."

At the shops, Tessa urged Rachael to pick out clothes, hats, shoes. What Rachael always wanted was books. But there were never any books in the stores Tessa took them to. So the little girl stayed silent and Tessa bought her flouncy dresses with ruffles and sashes, frilly anklets, patent leather shoes. Rachael liked herself plain—in jumpers, cotton shirts, kneesocks, loafers. In Tessa's clothes, Rachael felt like a carnival girl. In restaurants and parlors, dressed this way, Rachael was humiliated as Tessa paraded her around a room, visiting and talking at the other tables.

"My great niece," Tessa would say, presenting Rachael to the strangers, "my newest little guest." Rachael felt the invading stares of these strangers hot on her face; her body tensed into hardness. "Her mother's the one married to the soldier," Tessa said in a lowered voice, and Rachael's face burned. She knew her great-aunt meant *the poor ones, the ones who'd never live in houses like ours, eat in restaurants like these.*

Rachael hated her great-aunt's show of charity, hated even more the things she lied about. Rachael wished she could blurt out her aunt's fears and secrets. But Rachael felt ridiculous in her clothes, felt her tongue swelling with shame in her throat. She longed to say, "My father's an officer," which he was now. Her mother had told her so. "Your daddy's a Special Forces officer, honey. He's not some low-level soldier no more. Don't you listen when Aunt Tessa says that. It ain't true."

Rachael thought Bragg was a funny name but that was where her daddy was. Still, she wanted them all to be there together, like her mother said they would, once the housing came up. They could be happy then, her mother said. There, Rachael hoped she could say whatever she needed to say. But here at Tessa's elbow, Rachael stood choked by humiliation of how her body didn't feel like her own, of how she looked in those stupid frilly clothes. She hated the way all those fancy people looked at her. She clutched her doll, Miss Huggins, close to her chest.

The one gift Tessa bought for her that Rachael truly loved, Miss Huggins was a kind of fancy rag doll that matched the child's size, with elastic straps attached to its feet that fit beneath Rachael's shoes. The day they found her, Tessa had a sales clerk climb up a tall wooden ladder and bring the doll down. The doll sat on a shelf so high above their heads that she nearly touched the ceiling in the dusty old toy store. Rachael felt an immediate love for the doll and watched as the man carried it, limp and helpless in the crook of his left arm, as he descended rung by rung to the floor. When the doll was in her arms, Rachael clutched hard, feeling tears at the edges of her eyes. "You're safe now," she whispered.

Rachael called the doll Miss Huggins, because she loved to hug her with all her might, and vowed to take her everywhere with them.

"That's no babydoll, you know," Tessa told her. "You don't love her like a mommy."

"I know," Rachael said.

Tessa smiled. "Good," she said. "That's good."

They lay that night with the doll between them on their bed piled high with quilts and pillows. They snuggled beneath the blankets, washed in the blue light of the TV. Rachael fought to stay awake as they watched a bald-headed man named President Eisenhower tell them, "You have a row of dominoes set up. You knock over the first one, and what will happen to the last one is the certainty that it will go over very quickly."

"I wish you could stay with me forever," Tessa said.

Rachael didn't answer. She was already asleep.

Tessa stared long at the little girl; she studied how her tiny arms hugged the doll innocently to her side. Then she pulled the blankets up over her shoulders and turned to look at the photograph of herself that stood on the nightstand. Taken in Havana in 1946, it showed a younger Tessa, hand on hip, knee bent in a flirt's pose, in platform shoes and painted toenails, dark hair piled high, Cuban-style. Behind her loomed the famous Hotel Nacional, where inside at that same moment Biagio met secretly with Meyer Lansky and Lucky Luciano, planning things she knew not to ask about.

ELEANOR MEADE STOOD at the door of the run-down rental at 723 Piety Street wearing a frayed blue cotton night-gown ripped on the left collarbone. It was three in the afternoon. She fidgeted with the bobby pins that crisscrossed the rolled lumps of bleached hair on her head and watched the dark red Riviera with its long shark fins coast to a stop. She waited while Tessa and her little girl carried bags and boxes to the door. Rachael held Miss Huggins. When Tessa and Rachael approached, she motioned them inside quickly, as if they were being watched.

"I need to know why she wasn't home sooner," she said.

"Really?" Tessa handed her a shopping bag. "What do you have to know for?"

"Because she's missing too much school, Aunt Tessa."

The little girl looked quickly at her great-aunt. "You said she told me to stay."

Tessa just smiled at the child as she untied the silk scarf around her hair.

"Rachael's too smart for school," she said. "Isn't she only five in the first grade? She can take time away and still be smarter than all the rest."

As they entered the kitchen, Eleanor leaned down to look at her daughter's face more closely. "And it don't look right for her to be wearing all that makeup, either," she said. "Honey, go on to the bathroom and wash that off."

Tessa sat down at a chair near the kitchen table and took the child onto her lap. "Eleanor, Christ Almighty, you wore it too, at that same age."

"When?" Eleanor asked, puzzled.

"Every time I had you with me."

"Well my mother should've told you to stop painting my face," Eleanor said.

Rachael tried to slide off Tessa's lap, to go wash up the way her mother asked. But Tessa held her tighter. "Whoever loved you better than me, Ellie?" Tessa said, quietly.

A look of confusion moved across Eleanor's face. "What?" she said, her eyes darting nervously around the room.

"Your pious mother? Your beer-soaked father? Roy Meade, that soldier-boy husband?"

"I don't know," Eleanor said, closing her eyes.

She looked to Rachael as though she were struggling to think something through. The child watched her mother: her swollen face and unwashed pinned-up hair, its dark roots turning suddenly to a sort of lemon pie yellow. Her belly was bigger now, too. She moved even more slowly, with the baby coming soon. Rachael wanted her mom to be fixed up pretty like Tessa, to have her hair done up at the beauty salon, and wear makeup and perfume and new clothes from the shops. She wanted Tessa to take both of them to Esplanade Avenue, so her mom could be with them in her big home with the tall windows and the porch that wrapped around the house like a hug. She wanted her mom to sleep in a fancy room with her, and have Tildie bring them beignets and café au lait in the mornings. She would tell her mom about the whispered prayers and the brown-skinned man and the way Aunt Tessa lied about bananas and other things.

But Tessa's expression toward Eleanor was cold. "When did I ever hurt you," she asked. "When did I ever do anything but what you wanted me to?"

Eleanor kept her eyes closed and shook her head, as if to dislodge something. "I can't think right now," she began.

"Of course not," Tessa interrupted. "Not in this pigsty." She motioned to the upturned pile of unwashed dishes in the sink, the counter covered with dirty laundry. "What's happened to you? Why don't you do something about yourself? You're a god-awful mess."

Eleanor began to cry. "How can you say these hurtful things? There's nothing left of me, Aunt Tessa. I'm sick all day long. Roy's far away all these months. . . ."

Rachael jumped from her aunt's lap and ran to her mother. She put her arms around her mother's rounded body, trying to pat her back with her tiny hand.

"Your mother doesn't need you, Rachael," Tessa said sharply. "She got herself with another baby now."

"Don't say that to her," Eleanor said. "Rachael, honey, mommy loves you."

"Rachael needs to be with me," Tessa said. She turned to the little girl and smiled. "You'll help your mommy by staying with me, won't you my sweetheart?"

"I want her to come, too," Rachael said. "You have room."

"No," Tessa said quickly. "We'll give mommy money to fix this place up, and take better care of herself. Won't that be better?" She reached for Rachael's hand and drew her closer.

"I don't know," Rachael said, looking toward Eleanor.

"It is better," Tessa smiled. "And you'll be happier with me." She stroked Rachael's long black hair. "Nobody loves a little girl like I do."

Eleanor began to cry harder, wiping her eyes with an egg-stained dishcloth and turning her face away.

"Just stop this right now," Tessa hissed. "You'd think somebody was being killed here."

Eleanor straightened and sniffed, "I'm sorry, Aunt Tessa."

Tessa drew Rachael closer to her, never taking her eyes off Eleanor. "Well, that's better," she said. "Now get my purse."

Eleanor stared at Tessa, slightly dazed, "I don't want to," she whispered. "I want Rachael home now."

"What's the matter with you, Ellie?" Tessa said.

"I don't know," Eleanor began.

"Whose house is this?" Tessa asked. "Who lives here rent-free?"

"I know it's yours," Eleanor said, "and I'm grateful."

"Then prove it."

Rachael watched her mother, who only hung her head and didn't speak.

"Take the money, Eleanor," Tessa said. "For that new baby that's coming."

Eleanor went to the purse and removed a large roll of bills wrapped in a rubber band, closing her fingers around the money without looking at it. Rachael stared at her mother's hands. They were red and chapped. Her fingernails were bitten and bleeding.

"Take off the band," Tessa said sharply, "and take whatever you need to be happy again."

Eleanor stared straight ahead, dreamlike, peeling the bills off the roll slowly, breathing like she was pulling the bandage off an unhealed wound.

Watching her mother, Rachael went limp in her legs, and a shaking began in her stomach.

"What do you say, Ellie?" Tessa prodded.

Eleanor pushed the wad of bills into her nightgown pocket. "Thank you," she said flatly, handing the rest of the roll back.

Tessa smiled. "Good," she said. "Now doesn't that feel better?"

Eleanor's eyes were red. "You have to bring her home sometimes. She's my little girl."

"Sometimes?" Tessa said lightly. "Well, I guess that's all right."

Eleanor didn't answer. She moved toward Rachael and tried to take her hand. The child reached back to hold her mother, but Tessa's grasp tightened.

"You know I love you, Ellie," Tessa said. "And my money is yours, as long as there's no more of this stupidness."

Rachael felt the heaviness of her mother's quiet as she sat in this tiny kitchen. Outside the back door, an alley snaked behind cramped houses with collapsed porches and torn screen doors. Mangy, torn-up cats broken of their instinct watched rats feed themselves on sad, discarded spillage. The smells of mean living puckered the air they breathed here, and rain, when it came, fell greasy and useless to the ground. The child knew she was going back to Esplanade. Her heart suffered knowing Eleanor would stay behind, sitting alone in this kitchen when night came while Rachael would lie in that giant feather bed. The child knew that when sounds from the streets here turned frightening with voices and breakage in the dark, things on Esplanade would feel frozen by a magic spell, silent as a secret or a dream.

Rachael broke free from Tessa's hold and lifted Miss Huggins from the table. She carried the doll to her mother. "I want you to have her, mommy," she said. "She's a girl doll, not a baby. She's like me."

BACK ON ESPLANADE, Rachael wandered the house when Tessa took her afternoon rest. Tildie was in the kitchen, brewing coffee with chicory and humming to herself.

"Does he really eat those bananas?" Rachael asked, watching her.

Tildie's eyes flashed at the child quickly and, at first, she didn't answer. But slowly, she turned away from the stove and knelt down, motioning for Rachael to come toward her.

"It's how he get the energy for what he have to do," she said.

Rachael didn't answer. She stared into Tildie's face, which was soft and pretty, and saw in her eyes that she didn't need to be afraid.

"Miz Vitale know 'bout that statue in the bushes?" Tildie asked her.

Rachael shook her head, no. "Is he Uncle Biagio?" she asked.

Tildie's laughter rang softly through the room. "Oh, child, you do make me wonder," she said. "That's Ougo-Shango. He's big power. Gets inside anybody he want."

She removed the necklace that hung around her neck, a string of alternating red and white beads, and put them on the child. "Wear his colors. Don't ever take these off, you hear?" she said. "And he'll always keep protectin' you."

Rachael looked at her, wondering. "Tildie, are there really arms and legs flying?"

Tildie smiled at the little girl. "Only in the mind of the one he's been huntin'," she whispered.

Tessa had a shoebox hidden in her dressing closet, full of faded pictures from long ago. She showed them to Rachael and told her stories of her time as an orphan on the streets of the French Quarter.

"Who took care of you?" Rachael asked.

"No one," Tessa said.

"Where was your mommy?" Rachael asked.

"I killed her," Tessa said calmly, still looking through the photographs.

Rachael looked at her great-aunt's face, searching for the truth.

"Babies kill their mommas sometimes just gettin' born," Tessa said. "Like this new baby could kill your mama."

"You're lying," Rachael whispered.

Tessa shook her head.

"I don't want my mommy to die," Rachael said, beginning to cry.

"But God might," Tessa said. "He might just take her right back up to Heaven like he did with my momma. And then you would have to be my little girl instead."

"I want to go home," Rachael said, still crying. "I don't want anything bad to happen."

Tessa's laugh was a surprise. "Oh, Rachael. So many things can happen in the world. Especially to a girl with no parents to protect her."

She reached out to smooth the little girl's pajamas, running the palm of her hand slowly across the child's shoulder. She stroked Rachael's long hair again. "It's time for you to be my best girl, and come on to bed."

Rachael let her aunt help her back onto the big four-poster, and settled herself on the pillows. Her aunt lay down beside her, the crescendo of cicadas still rattling the air.

"It's going to rain," she said. "We need to go to the closet."

"There's not a cloud in the sky," Tessa said.

"I want Miss Huggins," Rachael said.

"Close your eyes," Tessa said, reaching out to pat her shoulder.

Rachael moved away. "I don't want to," she said.

Tessa tickled her niece softly on the back. "Honey, you know you have to listen to me now."

Rachael stayed quiet, holding herself very still.

"Who always takes care of you?" Tessa asked, running her polished nails softly across the child's face, down the tiny neck.

"You do," Rachael whispered. She could hear a distant rumbling outside the window.

"Whoever loves you more than me?"

"Nobody," Rachael said.

"Are you going to be my best girl now?" Tessa asked.

Rachael nodded her head, but couldn't speak, because Tessa's hand had traveled to where she knew it would go, into that place she didn't want it to be, where the fingers always made her body shake.

"There's my best girl," her aunt whispered. "I've found where I love her most of all."

Rachael hid behind her eyes whenever this thing happened, not wanting to be inside her body when it felt those fingers that never stopped, that kept drawing her to that churning place, where pieces of herself were roiled away. The first time this happened, Rachael went outside herself. She didn't know how, it just happened. From somewhere above, she saw a little body that seemed like someone else's, that seemed very far away, cradled in Tessa's arms. When Rachael floated back down inside herself, she was not the same as she used to be. Now all of her would always be hiding, crowded beneath the top of her skull, crouched behind her eyes, flattened behind the inside of her face. Everything else that used to be her felt dead. But Tessa nestled this new Rachael in her arms happily, and whispered, "Now you can be my best girl. Now you can belong to me forever."

Rachael was sick after that, and no one seemed to know what it was. Back home, she tried to tell her mother that she wasn't able to think, and that inside her, it felt like she would lift right out of her body and go away.

"Hush up," Eleanor said, fearfully. "Don't ever talk like that again. They'll think you're crazy and lock you away."

But it started happening at other times whenever Rachael got scared. She'd feel herself begin to go, and wouldn't be able to stop it. It happened at George Washington Elementary, during a test about volcanoes that Rachael was frightened about. Tessa had kept her out of school too long and she didn't know the answers. The teacher sent her to the nurse, who sent her to the school doctor. The school required tests, and in the hospital, the doctors stuck needles in her head that were attached to a metal machine. The needles kept falling out, and they kept stabbing them back in, while telling Rachael to lie still and not cry. The wires sent signals to the machine, which read her brain waves. When the tests were finished and reviewed, the doctors said it was petit mal. The doctors prescribed Phenobarbital pills.

Eleanor gave Rachael the pills for a while, then threw them away instead.

"You don't need no pills," she said. "This just runs in the family. You have to learn to hide it is all."

So Rachael found no help. And back on Esplanade, there was no choice but to give herself up to Tessa without a struggle. Each time she passed into her waking dream, Rachael knew that when Tessa asked, "Whoever loves you as much as me?" she should whisper, "Nobody."

And when Tessa said, "Will you ever feel this good without me?" she had to promise, "Never. I never will."

"You are my gentle little lamb," Tessa would sigh.

But Rachael was never really there. She felt nothing as she hid within the rush of wind that carried her outside her head. And from outside herself when she opened her eyes she saw spirits and angels, hovering around her in the air.

DOMINOES. THE INEVITABILITY of something set in motion. The knowledge that, once begun, all will fall in a predetermined way, until the last piece has toppled. On the island of Cuba tensions were high. Castro, freed from prison, was plotting revolution as he hid in the hills of Mexico. Biagio boarded a flight to New Orleans. Arriving in the middle of the night, he let himself quietly into the house on Esplanade as lightning flashed in the humid air outside. He moved through the dark to the bedroom where he stood staring at Tessa and Rachael asleep, his shadow enormous against the wall.

Rachael woke to their voices, urgent, arguing in strange whispered words that she didn't know were Italian. She saw Tessa sitting only in her panties, her arms across her breasts, her face averted from this swarthy man, who Rachael guessed was the uncle from the photographs, with his face turned fiercely toward his wife.

When he saw Rachael awake, Biagio stalked toward her. And when she looked up, afraid, her uncle was leaning over her, his eyes boring into hers.

"Have you become her zombie, little one?" he whispered, pulling her to standing, staring at her face and naked body. "Has she performed her voodoo on your soul?"

Rachael couldn't look away quickly enough and he read there in her face what he expected to, letting her drop back onto the blankets in disgust. He looked again at Tessa, with the flame of rage in his eyes. He led Rachael quickly to another room and left her alone there, huddled beneath the blankets. She listened to the angry words that volleyed through the night, and to other sounds she couldn't understand, which made her as afraid as she had ever been.

In the morning, Tessa's face was swollen and bruised, and she wouldn't meet Rachael's eyes. "Gio says you're a monster," she said, "that you have to stay home with your mother for good."

A pain started sharply in the child's head and traveled quickly to her chest, twisting itself through her heart. "But why?" she stammered. The salty taste of tears rose in her mouth.

"Everything would have been fine, Rachael," Tessa said. "But you let him see. A man must never see. It makes him think he has to do something."

Rachael didn't understand. She stared at her aunt, who would not look back at her. She wanted to go home. She wanted her mother. But she didn't want to be a monster.

"Just remember, Rachael, it was you who said yes every time. It was you. I only did what you asked me to do."

"Can I still be your best, Aunt Tessa?" Rachael choked, her eyes burning.

Tessa looked angrily into the small, upturned face. Her own right eye was swollen shut, and her lower lip was split. "Look what you made him do to me," she said. "You ruined everything. You can never be my best anymore."

So, Rachael found herself home on Piety Street. Secretly, she searched her face in the mirror, worried there were signs of wickedness on her that anyone might see, but not knowing what they could be. If the Army saw them at Bragg, they'd make her daddy send her away.

In her room at night, she lay awake staring at the circus figures on her wallpaper whose faces turned evil in the dark, whose bodies seemed to split into pieces and dance across the walls and ceiling. Her new sister cried in the crib in the room next door, and Rachael's heart pounded hard and fast in her chest. The sounds outside her window broke the night. Curses and bottles shattered, forces moved dangerously around them in the dark. It felt like she couldn't breathe in the right way, like she couldn't remember how to inhale.

One day she stood at the door, hoping Tessa might come back and tell her Biagio was wrong, that she wasn't a monster, that she was good.

Her mother stood behind her. "Get away from the door," she said.

Rachael turned and looked at her mother carefully. Eleanor held the baby in her arms and would not look into her daughter's face.

"You're not going no more," she said. "It's over. Be thankful."

"If I say I'm sorry," Rachael said. "If I see her again to say I'm sorry, she'll say I'm not a monster."

Eleanor stiffened. "Put it behind you, Rachael," she said. "Never even think about it."

"But she loves me, mom," Rachael said. "Don't you remember? She said I was her best."

Eleanor's hand came down hard, stinging Rachael's cheek and lip. The baby began to cry.

"Did I raise a fool?" she hissed, grabbing her daughter's face and wrenching it toward her. The baby howled on her other arm. "Do you think you're the only one she's said it to?"

THE ARMY MOVED THEM to Fort Bragg at the New Year. It was an army city. Camouflaged jeeps and trucks rolled by. Men in green uniforms and gleaming black boots moved quickly with purpose through the streets. Nobody cursed here, or broke bottles in the night. It was cleaner than on Piety Street. There was grass, large stretches of it, all around the houses.

There were trimmed shrubs. Their new house had three bedrooms and a backyard with a barbecue grill and a place for a garden once spring came. Rachael told her daddy that she wanted to plant a tumble of red roses and put bananas beneath them.

"Hush your nonsense, Rachael Meade," Eleanor said.

Next door, in a house attached to theirs, was a family with two boys, Vince Jr. and Pauly, who taught Rachael how to play Statue and King of the Mountain. Their dad, Vince Sr., had been in Korea with Roy; this was a place far away where, they told her, they had jumped from planes and floated with parachutes that looked like clouds in the sky. She wanted to ask them if they saw her angels, but was afraid of what her mother would say. Vince's wife was named Hedy. She was red-haired and pretty, with a funny accent from a place called Pittsburgh that Eleanor told Rachael was "way high up north." Rachael liked her immediately and wondered if she could fly.

Rachael got to go to a new school there on base, where the teachers recognized her intelligence right away and hung her papers on the bulletin board with red and gold stars sprinkled over them. All the kids who went there had dads in the Army, and Rachael worked really hard to show everyone she was good, and she was smart, and that she would never forget her homework or do anything like a monster would do. Sometimes Hedy would even take her to church with Vince and Pauly, and she'd get to sit in Sunday School and hear about the ascension of Jesus and his mother, or about the war of angels in heaven, and then color a picture she'd carry home and tape to the door of her bedroom closet, thinking all these good things carried a special kind of magic that would flow over her while she slept, turning her back into someone who was good again.

Dominoes. From a silenced mahogany table in Geneva where a line had been drawn cutting a place called Vietnam in half, to a day in June when Roy shipped out to Fort Shafter in Hawaii. He and Vince both went in a group called the 8251st Army Service Unit, a cover name which fooled no one. This was really the 14th Special Forces Operational Detachment, and soon they'd be sent to Thailand, Taiwan and Vietnam, where the Special Forces would stay for the next twenty years.

With Roy gone to Vietnam, Eleanor spent day after day crying and not getting out of her bed. Since it was summertime and she had no school, Rachael cared for her little sister as best she could. She fixed them both Gerber Baby Cereal that she found in an unpacked kitchen box, whispering secret words and crushing eggshells into the bowl. She dressed them from the boxes still stacked in the bedrooms and wore Tildie's special secret beads each and every day.

Time began to pass. This new world would take Rachael spinning away. Buried deep within her mind a veil of secrecy would fall. Lightly at first, the veil would settle more heavily in time, wrapping itself around those memories of Esplanade Avenue, leaving a fog which drifted like darkness over everything, burying all beneath a vague confusion.

One day, up in the attic searching for the things she needed most, Rachael found Miss Huggins. The doll was sitting beneath the eaves in the attic, on top of a box of frilly party dresses. The child lifted the doll gently and held her to her chest.

"You are my favorite," she said rocking her gently. Tears sprang to her eyes and a warm flush of something disturbing made her heart flutter, briefly. Somewhere in her mind there was thunder and a rush of fear. Rachael stood carefully, holding the light weight of the doll's soft body against hers as she stretched to her full height. Up there where the eaves nearly touched the summer sky, where she knew her angels and spirits would always be, she felt something familiar, something strong. She felt ready, somehow, to begin.

All the Accidents of Man

IN AUGUST OF '59, our home in Alabama burned, not badly, but just enough that we had to move. It was a fast fire that my brother Martin and I saw blaze through most of the first floor and part of the second. We sat watching the firemen pull hoses across our lawn, listening to their yells and to the sounds of shattering glass above the roar of the water.

Neighbors gathered in small groups on the sidewalk across the street. They stood watching calmly, talking together, measuring the fire's effect. Not one among them approached our family.

Our father was in a rage, throwing armloads of sopping, unrecognizable stuff from the house into the back of our station wagon. At first, our mother yelled for him to stop, her voice rising into the night. But shouting made her ashamed, and she stopped quickly, her face turning hard and fierce in its silence. She sat on the wet sidewalk hugging her legs until dawn approached, staring mutely as the firemen pulled their hoses up and packed their equipment into the truck. My brother, who was seven, had pieced together some information and explained it to me.

"Dad says we're bankrobbed," he said, "unless we go to the beach."

This all sounded fine to me and I started to yell hooray, but one glance at my mother's swollen, angry eyes stopped me mid-holler. That's when she pulled me to her, hard.

"Marlena, don't let anything or anybody stop you from doin' what you feel," she said. "Just go on and yell if you want to."

"I don't need to, mommy," I said. "It's okay."

She knelt down and drew us both to her, Martin and me, looking secretively in the direction of my father.

"This was nobody's fault," she whispered. "Not yours. Not mine. The firemen said so. Do you understand?"

We both nodded, feeling her arms around our backs, her protection against whatever truths were hid.

After the firetrucks pulled away down the street, my father stormed toward us and, without breaking stride, hoisted Martin and me up into his arms. He dumped us into the back of the car on top of the wet piles. My mother climbed silently into the front seat and my dad floored the gas, burning tire marks all the way off the street. We were leaving the house charred, drenched and abandoned behind us. He didn't care that my brother and I were looking, but when our mother turned to watch the house shrink in the distance, he roared, "You face forward, goddamn you!"

"Don't you try blaming me for this, Vince," she said.

Like a flash, he yanked a handful of her hair, whipping her head toward him and swerving down the road. "How the hell you gonna stop me, Ronnie?" he said.

She didn't answer, and he let her go, giving her head a snap. She regained her balance and stared straight ahead without speaking. Martin and I knew enough to stay quiet, too, but I risked patting the back of my mom's neck on and off through the next few hours, most of the way to Florida.

We drove to Wellerton, and what I first saw of the old town was flattered by early light. Off the main route now, we rode through streets of well-kept two-story houses. I remember them as being bathed in cool morning sun; gingerbread woodwork and wicker porch swings were still dappled in shade; I believe I saw dew clinging to flowering plants on porches and at window boxes.

I remember that I said, "I like it here, dad," and that my father's shoulders stiffened. Martin put his hand over mine and shot a dark warning from his eyes. I looked down at my knees until the danger passed and didn't talk again.

We drove on and the rising sun evaporated the freshness. The houses became newer and lost their charm. Finally, houses stopped altogether and we drove on a sand-packed road, past a trailer park and a billboard big as an outdoor movie screen that said, "Welcome to Wellerton Beach!" in large sky-blue letters. The billboard pictured a giant woman, wearing a yellow one-piece bathing suit and matching hairband. Her hair flipped up on the ends, all around. She held a beachball like it was the world at her fingertips and the smile she flashed in our direction was totally without insight.

Beyond the billboard, newly-built beach cottages, identical and undersized, sat lined up like Monopoly houses around machine-dug lagoons. The lagoons were filled with sea water captured mid-flow on its way to St. Andrew's Bay. This was where, a year before, my father's parents had put a hundred dollars down and moved into a two-bedroom bungalow.

Our car tires crunched on the stones of the driveway as we pulled up to their back door. My father cut the motor and sat silently for a minute.

"Life in a shingled box," my mother said, her first words since we left Alabama. "If you can do better, go do it," my father snapped.

They were silent again.

My father went alone to the house. He stood talking to our grandfather, who had answered his knock and now listened behind the screen door to whatever my father was telling him. When he opened the door to let my father in, no one motioned for us to follow. So we waited in the car, feeling the heat of the day rise even more. The wet heap we sat on throughout the ride had soaked our pajamas through, and was now giving off a sour smell. The dank odor clung to our wet and wrinkled fingers and feet.

Martin and I concentrated on the gulls, their silver-white bodies streaking quickly into the sky, then diving down to skim the water. Sometimes one would perch itself on a pillar of the docks that lined the lagoons. My mother paid no attention. She took down and braided her hair, which was long and black and soft as silk. Then she pinned it up again, sticking the pins into her hair with rapid, sharp motions that made me wince.

After a long time, my grandmother came, and stared through the screen door. Thinking back, I know she stood there long enough to make it clear to my mother that she didn't want to come out, and then she came out. She walked with little, heavy steps across the sand to my mother's side of the car, opened the door and stepped back quickly.

"This is going to be something of a squeeze," she said.

In the days that followed we tried to salvage what we could. Dad emptied out the car, and we hung our wet belongings on the clothesline, draped them across the sand, spread them on the cement porch, for the sun to bake dry. A lot of what my father brought he brought in a fury, so what we were left with made no sense: clothes we had already grown out of, shoes with no mates, catfood for a pet long dead.

My grandfather emptied out a large pantry closet and pushed a bunkbed into the space. My father removed the door from its hinges and hung a curtain over the opening. This was where Martin and I slept, and we loved it. The very best thing about sleeping there was that the grownups forgot we were only behind a curtain, not a door, and that we could hear everything they did or said. We would lie still and listen, trying to imagine their actions by the sounds we heard. As for conversations, what few there were, Martin explained those to me with great authority and at times, I realize now, with great freedom from the constraints of fact.

My dad had just lost another construction job in Alabama before the house burned. So, it was actually better here, where he could work with his father and not worry about getting into his regular trouble. Here, he helped plaster houses for the town people of Wellerton, and for people in other places with names Martin and I loved to chant, like Choctawhatchee, Crooked Island, Dead Lake. We conjured Indian villages, beaches with twisted trees, spirits rising from the misty waters.

From our curtained beds off the kitchen, we'd listen for the sounds of the men waking at dawn, preparing themselves for travel toward the wonders we imagined. Martin played lookout and whenever it seemed safe, he'd peek out of the curtain, reporting, for instance, that they wore only socks and boxers in the kitchen. They stood, dressed in this peculiar way, and fixed their coffee at the counter. Sometimes they'd pour from the brown bottle grandfather kept under the sink right into their coffee. This was meant to be a secret, but grandmother sniffed at the cups they left behind each morning.

When they stirred cream into their coffee, the spoons would ring against the sides of the cups. By the sound of my grandfather's slurp, I knew he was drinking his coffee from the saucer, the way men like him feel driven to do when their women aren't around. I also knew he'd be rubbing the lump that bulged from the base of his neck the way he always rubbed it, without thinking. It was the size of a small melon, and forced his head forward a little ways. I couldn't look at it without having my stomach flutter.

Sometimes one of them, we couldn't always tell who, would make a low comment about the weather, the supplies, the job; sometimes the other would mutter a reply. Most times there wasn't any talk between them, and Martin and I could just lie quietly, figuring out from the different sounds they made how close they were to leaving. We knew they were very close when the footsteps shuffled to the back door. That was when they were pulling their plastering clothes off the back door hook and putting them on.

Washing couldn't remove all the hardened chunks of plaster, so grandmother wouldn't allow the clothes beyond that point. Their shoes were worse, and she made the men keep them on the patio. Walking in them sometimes broke loose a lump of plaster, and it would fall and shatter like a chunk of chalk, leaving a clinging white dust to whatever surface it met. In the dim of evening, Martin and I liked to slide our skinny, sun-browned legs into those shoes and clump around, making little bursts like explosions as we marched. We'd act out that we were the men, coming home. But the workboots came up to our knees and, most times, we would fall down laughing before we got the staggering right.

When the screen door slammed and they were finally gone, the silent house seemed to breathe in relief. We knew that our mother would soon be slipping quietly behind our curtain and sliding her brown bag of food supplies from its hiding place beneath my bunk. Quietly, she offered us dry cereal, Tang and bottled water in paper cups, sometimes peanut butter, to be eaten right from the jar on a shared plastic spoon. This was secret food which we ate quickly, but with a certain ceremony, as we sat wrapped in our bedsheets. It was our mother's food, and as young as we were, we knew not to speak of it outside of our curtained space. After returning the bag and its contents to its hiding place, our mother dressed and kissed us and sent us to our grandmother's table.

By then, grandmother was in the kitchen with the kettle whistling quietly, the frying pan sizzling. The milk and juice were poured, the toast was buttered, the muffins cut and spread with honey.

We ate this second breakfast seated at the table like normal children, and never let on how powerfully filled with mysteries we were. Even the fishing boats which sputtered past the end of the lagoon appeared mystical to us. Their wakes cut deep grooves in the water, and sparks of sunlight flashed on their chrome. Our hearts nearly burst with the sight of them as we imagined their voyages and adventures while eating and keeping our secrets.

If the silence of the men felt like religion to my brother and me, the silence of the women felt like war. They moved around each other, spoke around each other. They worked, never quite together, to keep house. Grandmother wore flower print dresses and amber beads. Even as young as I was, I felt this as an assault to my mother, who wore whatever she had left after the fire, pieces that didn't match the season or each other. It made her stay inside most times. She never got to be like the lady of the billboard.

"Why do you hate my mother?" I asked my grandmother one day.

She had been smoothing a bedspread across the pillows of her bed, and she straightened up, looking past me out the screened window, toward the lagoon.

"God tells us not to hate anyone, Marlena," she said. "And He knows how hard I try."

"How come He can't help you do better?"

My grandmother concentrated on tucking a piece of torn vinyl back into the seam of the headboard. "Because," she said, "I guess we're meant to suffer the consequences of what we fail to do."

"If you're the one who can't do better," I asked, "how come it's my mom who always cries?"

"Your mother cries because she married a man she had no right to marry," my grandmother said.

There's a picture I still have of my mom and dad, taken on the day of their wedding. They stood before a backdrop that looked like the room of a mansion. My mother's dress had padded shoulders and a gardenia corsage flowered so large that it covered her left breast completely. She towered over my father because she was wearing heels. My father, medium height and stocky, looked wide and squat in a double-breasted pin-stripe and black and white oxfords. Their bodies were posed at an angle. My father cupped my mother's elbow in his hand. Their faces were turned toward the camera. My mother's chin was high and her right eyebrow was raised. My father's face looked broad and flat, and his smile had too much amazement in it.

Once, I asked my mom how they got to be in that beautiful place.

"Things lead us to certain times, Marly," she said. "But they're no more important than the things that lead us away again."

I still don't know if that's true. As for the things that led my parents to each other, what I know now is where it started with my father. As a boy, it was his job to retrieve his own father from the taproom each night. He did it throughout his boyhood years, obedient to the demands of his mother, until the night he sat on a barstool, drank his first shot and quickly changed allegiances. My grandmother never forgave the betrayal, holding herself away from her only son from that day on with a silence more deadly than spoken hatred. My father saw no choice but to feed his father's new-formed affection by embracing his paternal traditions of alcoholism and riotous behavior. And he took to it quickly. By the time he was nineteen, he was a magnificent drunk.

It was on one of those drunken nights that he stumbled through the door of the Paradise Diner, colliding into a waitress who would someday be my mother, sending her and a tray of food crashing to the floor.

Without speaking a word, they reached out toward each other, removing shards of glass and debris from the other's clothes and face. When the owner of the diner had him jailed, my mother bailed him out with tip money pooled from all the waitresses, and that's how they started.

I don't know much about where my mother's story starts. But she was 17 when it intersected with my father's, and by then she was already strong and secretive and exotically beautiful. My father, starved as he was for woman's love, proposed to her every day for two months. I don't know what made her say yes at the end, but she did, and they were married, alone, in the office of a Justice of the Peace. That was where they paid a photographer to snap their picture, standing before that hazy winding-staircase-of-the-mansion backdrop, looking to the camera as if it were the future.

A year went by well enough, with my father sober and my mother happy. They might have felt the stirrings of hope during that time, maybe even coming to believe in the possibilities of the future. They wouldn't have suspected that, at the end of that year, when my brother was born, he would not be a Caucasian child.

What my father had never learned in all those days of proposing was that my mother was the daughter of a whore who still lived and worked outside Dennersfield. My mother was the oldest of her four children—each obviously the result of some omission or misapplication. None of the woman's children knew who their fathers might have been, but my mother never suspected that, in her dark look and tawny skin, there lay the blood of a race which would shatter all the pieces of truth she had strung together, and ruin all her dreams of innocent happiness. It was 1952, and no one pretended that there was such a thing as racial harmony.

It was also a time when women slept, drugged, through the birth of their children, and fathers were sequestered in waiting rooms.

On the night Martin was born, there was a great horror among those working in Delivery. One look at his wooly hair and maple-colored skin, and they realized that this child and his mother had to be moved quickly to the Negro hospital across town. I can only imagine how disrespectfully they rolled my sleeping mother into the hall for transport, how hurriedly they changed the forms and murmured to one another. I don't know what my father thought or felt, or how he looked, as the doctor informed him. But I do imagine him raging like an animal at what he was told, knocking aside the doctor and anyone else who got in his way, fighting his way to my mother. Whether his fighting was to save her or to destroy her I never can decide.

But this is where my imagining fails me most. What could my mother have felt, being shaken, still drugged, being forced to hear words and see a child that her mind was too numb to understand the meaning of? Did she turn away from my brother and scream? Did my brother stiffen and shriek in a nurse's hands? Or did my mother, in her dream-like haze, still cradle Martin as something precious and apart from this sudden truth, did she refuse in spite of it all to allow her moment of sweet new motherhood to be wrestled away?

I know my father moved the family out of Eufaula. But he only took them as far as the outskirts, to a patchy kind of nonplace called Gretna, where he hoped they'd be left in peace. To his credit, my father never once left my mother or Martin. All the same, his fury was relentless. Even when he tried to hold it down, it rose to tear at all of them. He may have tried to love my brother. Or, maybe it didn't cross his mind. I believe he still loved my mother, but not with a love of expectation or peace. This love looked over its shoulder in shame, expecting the worst, mocking itself. His drinking began again and became monstrous; as it loomed larger, it left less and less space for any kind of hope at all.

Things went on, though, and two years later I was born, wheat-blonde, but golden skinned, with features vaguely Asian.

"This one's a fuckin' tepee dweller," was my father's response.

Down in Wellerton, my grandmother called me "Minni-haha" and said I should wear a feather in my hair. She could barely look at Martin, calling him "Li'l Black Sambo" under her breath as his skin darkened to the color of molasses in the summer sun. Our mother assured him that this nickname had something to do with his love of pancakes.

To my grandmother, my mother said, "My children have names, and I want you to use them."

"Who are you to make demands?" my grandmother said. "You should kiss the ground I walk on for allowing any of you here."

My grandfather never called us anything. He spoke to no one but my father, and that only occasionally. Still, it was he, on one of those occasional times, who told my father one of my mother's secrets, that she was leaving in the early hours of the morning and staying out until nearly dawn. He said it one morning while they stirred their coffee and I listened behind the curtain.

"That woman you got hauled herself outa here 'round one this morning, didn't get back 'til daybreak," is what he said, exactly.

I peeked out of the curtain right away when I heard that, and saw him sitting with his back toward me. The lump at the base of his neck swelled beneath his undershirt as he breathed.

My father never looked up from his coffee, never answered. But I knew he'd have my mother out on the dock that night to speak about it. That was where they went when they needed to be private. Sometimes if I knew they were going, I'd have just enough time to climb under the dock and listen. Martin had taught me how to do it. I would crouch on the bank where it rose just above the water line, and dig my fingers deeply into the spongy muck to keep myself from sliding into the water. This night I got there just in time before my parents' feet sounded on the boards above me. I watched their shadows flicker down through the slats of wood and float on the moonlit water as it rolled over my bare toes. It was hard for my father to ask her, and he stumbled through his words.

"I won't ask you the why of it," he said, finally. "But you owe me to say who you're going to see."

"It's not meant to cost you," was all she answered.

My father didn't talk again right away, and when he did his voice had changed to something thicker than before, so that his words bubbled through and broke surface.

"Everything you do, Ronnie," he whispered. "Every goddamned thing you do."

I knew even then he didn't understand enough of anything to ask her the right questions, and I think he knew it too.

But I knew where she went, even if my father didn't, because after a while she started taking Martin and me with her.

She'd fill the back of the station wagon with blankets and pillows and carry us out in the early morning hours. She'd drive and we'd fall back to sleep. Sometimes she would only drive through the backroads of the forest, and we would wake to see the dark sky and its stars through the window of the back. Other times we would wake up in the driveway of our Gretna house. The overgrown grass, the dirty windows, the weeds growing up between the cracks where the firetrucks split the driveway made it look as if no one had ever lived there or could live there again. Sometimes our mother let us out of the car to run through the backyard in the moonlight. She stayed inside the house, trying her best to put things back together. We lay on the grass outside looking up at the constellations; we ate doughnuts from a box and drank orange juice from a carton. Martin swallowed his right down, but I took small bites, chewing slowly, feeling the tightness of my throat as a warning that this was the night my mother could find some evidence against me, proof of a guilt I couldn't specify, something that would cause her to take her love away. But each time, the sky would begin to lighten, and mom would tuck us into the back of the wagon, heading south toward the Gulf again. If she ever found a reason to deny me her tenderness, she never said a thing about it.

When my mother found that another baby was coming, the rides got more frequent, the trips home more regular. It got so that Martin and I spent more nights getting our whole night's sleep in the back of the wagon. Sometimes we never woke at all. But my mother, sleeping less and less, would wander our empty house for hours alone, sometimes working, sometimes eating the canned or packaged food left in the cupboards, drinking the instant coffee black in the left-behind mugs.

One time I woke up in the back of the wagon where it was left parked in the driveway, and saw her through the picture window. She wore canvas sneakers, old jeans and one of my father's shirts, knotted at the front. Her hair was in a ponytail and she held a coffee mug in her hand. A camping lantern flickered a bare yellow haze through the black and splashed her with different shades of light as she moved slowly about the room. It felt like I was watching a TV show, and I just sat there, as Martin slept beside me, staring into that window, watching a lonely woman who seemed for the first time to my startled eyes to be nobody's mother.

The rides stopped being a secret. My mom would carry the pillows and blankets to the back of the car in the broad daylight of mid-afternoon, so that Martin and I would know early on where our sleeping was going to be done that night. Sometimes Martin would say, "We're going to sleep twice as bad with a two-timing mother tonight," echoing a remark he heard our grandmother make. He liked to say it, I think, because at seven, he couldn't make sense of it, but it sounded magical and wondrous, as if this were one more proof that we lived an enchanted life.

One night in August, the heat was so bad that mom only packed bedsheets, no blankets, and said they'd feel cooler against our skin if we slept in our underwear and powdered up our legs and arms and necks. We did, and used up most of a can of talc until our skin was white, and the crevices where our arms folded were filled with lines of wet white dough. The back of the station wagon was foggy with the dust of the powder, and sweet with its smell. My hair and my brother's were powdered white. We looked ancient—eighty, ninety years old—wrapped in bleached white sheets that still held an odor of chlorine mixed with the aroma of our oatmeal cookies.

My mother was enormous now, and walked with a rolling motion. She had pinned her hair up with bobby pins and dabbed at her face and chest with a tissue. The cotton of her sack blouse was wrinkled and limp, and I could make out what I didn't know then was the bulge of her popped-out belly button.

We slept in powdered sweetness all through the ride across the black roads, through the black trees, under the black skies. My mother had cranked the big back window of the wagon down and opened all the car windows down to the door frames. As she drove, the radio played music that only she could hear, but the hint of sound that floated on the delicious wind of movement was enough to keep us peaceful in our dreams.

I don't know if we were headed home that night, or if my mother just planned to drive until daybreak through the forest roads. I don't know if she ever planned one or the other. On this night, though, the decision was made for her as a buck flung himself through the black, stifling air and landed— young, strong, expectant—right in the middle of Route 77. My mother had no time to stop or swerve. Her headlights dazzled him, stunned him so that he stopped stiff, mesmerized, staring straight into the brilliance that blinded him, and she barreled down on his stillness and collided.

Somehow our bodies, my brother's and mine, were thrown through the back of the wagon, through the opening of the back window, and we awoke already skidding through the forest tangles, still wrapped in bedsheets and covered with talc. The car, by the time we realized that we should look for it, must have skidded far into the woods where we, at seven and five, couldn't see, and where we were too terrified to go.

We were found crying at the side of the road by a couple who had heard the accident. They ran a motel a short walk down the highway, and gathered us to them without questioning—two children in underwear and sheets, powdered white and spotted with blood, whose footsteps sent little bursts of talc into the air as they stumbled in the darkness. One child was dark and thick as the night, the other as shimmering and thin as the crescent moon; both continued to cry and hold each other as they were led into a strange kitchen and sat at a dimly-lit table.

The couple fed us corn on the cob, chicken, milk, and several slices each of chocolate cake. Two State Policemen came into the kitchen where we sat eating and crying, and talked to the couple. They only looked at us a little, then left. The people finished feeding us, then made our beds on their sofa. One of the troopers returned to say that he found the buck, who had dragged himself off to the edge of a small lake within the woods and died, the hole in his side torn clean open to his organs, his head flopped sadly in a dark pool of liquid.

The car had traveled on for some distance and was found against a tree, in no condition to be salvaged. Its dashboard and front seat were scattered with bobby pins, glass and blood; no one was in the car.

After more searching, they found a woman. She was conscious, whimpering, bloody, under some brush off the other side of the road. It took them some time to realize she was giving birth, and they finally helped her in the last moments before dawn to deliver a baby girl who, the trooper said, had the biggest eyes he had ever seen in a child.

My mother named her Miranda Lynn. She was a beautiful baby, the most normal-looking of all of us, except for those eyes which, for her whole life, startled people into looking away from her face and then looking back to see what they saw again.

The troopers drove us home, and we arrived at the door just as the men were loading up the truck to head for work. The patrol car slowed to pull into the driveway and my grandfather took one look, turned his back and walked into the house. My father looked up and stiffened. He stared at the police car, his arms tightening around the tarp he was just about to throw onto the truck. As the trooper spoke, my father squinted so hard that his left eye twitched and blinked.

Finally, we were left out of the car, and my father lifted us both in one scoop, Martin and me and the sheets we were still wrapped in. He carried us into the house, and he stayed with us that whole day. One time I saw him look out the window and hold his head, as if his eyes hurt him dreadfully. His jaw muscles worked and worked, as if he was chewing something so terrible that he just didn't know how to swallow.

When my mother came home from the hospital, there was a different look to her face that Martin and I saw right away. We felt afraid when she stayed on the sofa, letting our grandmother tend us and the new baby. When grandmother called us by her nicknames, and when she began calling the baby Doe-Eyes, our mother showed no sign of hearing.

There was no more driving at night. There were no more secret breakfasts. Our mother went about tight-lipped and dry-eyed, tending us when she was finally able in a way she might have tended her half-brothers and sister before she passed out of their lives forever.

A very short time after that, my father moved us back to the house in Alabama. We never saw Wellerton or my grandparents again. Then, my father did an unexpected thing. He declared he would stop drinking.

"It's time I woke up, Ronnie," he said to my mother.

Martin and I thought this could be just the thing my mother needed, just the thing to bring back her strength and will. We stopped what we were doing and waited, watching her.

She was standing in the kitchen when he said it, with the baby crawling around her feet. She stood looking at the sincere expression on my father's face for a full minute. Then she began, very slowly, but with great strength and will, to break everything in the room. She broke chairs, she broke dishes, she broke windows. Then she broke every glass in the cupboard except for one, which she held in her hand. My father scooped Miranda into his arms and held her against his chest. My mother looked first at them, then at the glass, as if it were an artifact from a forgotten lifetime. At last, she opened her hand and let the glass drop. It was as if there was some kind of rupture within her, and that was all. The next morning she was gone.

The lives we lived went on without her because no one knew how to stop them. Our father retreated into drunken silence, and hoped we would leave him alone. He never spoke our mother's name again. Martin and I learned to speak of her only to each other, in secret ways.

"Peanut butter," he would whisper to me, holding up a plastic spoon.

"Tang," I would answer.

Miranda could only look from one to the other of us, knowing we hadn't enough power to initiate her in these mysteries. Far more devastating to my brother and me was the sorrow that, in the end, we hadn't done enough of whatever we should have done to make our mother stay.

When I was old enough to leave home, it seemed right to follow in my mother's footsteps, wherever they might lead. It wasn't so much that I expected to find her as that I hoped she'd reappear. I pinned up my hair, I drove until dawn, I did whatever I thought might conjure her. But nothing happened. It seemed I'd never found a way of being where my mother, too, might be. Sometimes I wondered, should I just forget she's out there. The distances between us, no matter what promise they held, extended beyond the lines of any map, in all and every infinite direction.

Instead, it was my father who appeared to me, in dreams. Always, my father: young, somehow strong, wrapped in a sheet and powdered. I approach and speak carefully, as if he is the master at the end of my long journey.

"I am traveling," I tell him, "the distance between a heart and its happiness."

He opens the sheet to reveal his rended flesh, a wide hole teeming with unimaginable sorrows.

"I am suffering," he shows me, "the wound of their mysterious collision."

A Kind of Heaven

We were living off post at Fort Bragg. I was twelve, home from school because of snow—something rare in those parts—when Nana Galloway showed up at our door. She was a sight, standing in a whirling storm with her matted fox-fur stole looped and dangling off her shoulders. Her grey hair beneath the pillbox hat was wet with the flakes still coming down. And she lifted a paper carry-all bag in each hand high above the frozen bushes beside our door.

My sister bounced on both feet beside me, twisting her shoulders back and forth, hoping these bags were filled with things for us. That's when my mother swooped down, lifting Midget's little dancing body with both hands and swinging my sister aside with her legs still jumping in the air.

"To your rooms NOW," she ordered. So I took Midget's hand and led her, as she hopped, just far enough up the stairs, to where I could peek around the wall and watch.

My mother glared over my grandmother's shoulder at a cab-driver, waiting to be paid. "Don't tell me you took a taxi from Panama City," she said.

"I got a flat rate, Eleanor," my grandmother said. "D'you expect me to walk hundreds of miles?"

The cabby had carried more paper bags into the livingroom and my sister and I watched from the step as Nana paid him, counting out five crisp bills and laying them flat in his palm. My mother stood with her arms folded across her cardigan, her eyes squinting and her lips pinched closed.

When the driver left, my mother closed the door and leaned against it.

"Did you once think of calling first?" she said.

"You'd only tell me not to come. You'd say the baby is sick. Rachael has asthma. Roy's taken another tour of duty."

"All of it's true," my mother said.

"Well, there's no heat in my house and your father's gone God-knows-where for days at a time."

"My husband's in the god-damn rice paddies, a letter every six months. Some people learn to live with things," my mother said.

She was lying. My mother liked it when my father was away. She had a harder time living between those tours of duty, when she struggled against my father to retain every ounce of her stateside power.

Nan seemed far away, not listening. She combed the fox-fur with her fingers. "They turned the water off yesterday," she said, hanging the stole in the closet. "That was the last straw."

"You should have called," my mother repeated. "I would have come to get you."

"Don't lie to me, Ellie. You don't want me here. Besides the fact that they turned the phone off last week."

"Do you realize how crazy you are? You can't pay bills but you pay a taxi to take you across state lines?"

"This is the money I hid," my grandmother said, holding her purse to her chest. "How can I keep it hid if I use it to pay bills?"

Midget pulled at my sleeve as we huddled together on the stairs.

"Rachael" she whispered.

"Shhh," I said. "I'm trying to hear."

"Them bags are for us?" she asked.

"No," I said. "It's all Nana's stuff. I think she's moving in." The bags had fallen on the livingroom rug, the contents a tumble of unmatched stockings, old lady underwear, unfolded flannel lumps of clothes.

"Uh-oh, that's bad," Midgy said. "That lady has no presents."

"That's Nana Galloway," I said. "She's our grandmother."

Midget's face was blank, reminding me that she was only four, too young to know the pictures in the album, the stories our mother told. But I wasn't. I knew what my mother was thinking at that very moment. I knew what she'd say about all those carry-all bags. It was the same theme all the time, that if my grandmother had married the right man, she'd have owned real luggage, instead of paper bags to cart her clothes in. She'd have owned real pearls instead of the glass beads she wore now. And she'd have sported something in the chill of February besides the ratty, motheaten, castoff stole she begged her neighbor not to throw away.

But this was the story my mother told me over and over, like a favorite fairy tale: Nana didn't marry the right man. She married my grandfather.

"If somebody'd been there to protect her, they'd have seen right away that Billy Galloway was nothin' but misery. They'd have known that the most treasured Galloway tradition was to become alcoholic before reaching the legal drinking age."

But my grandmother was alone, the older of two immigrant sisters orphaned by the influenza epidemic of 1918 and raised in a Catholic orphanage.

"Too little love and too much Catholicism," is how my mother explained her own mother's downfall. "One look at my father," she'd say, "and anyone else would know he was the kind of creature born to face down the power of Jesus."

But that didn't stop Lucia DiNobile, my grandmother. She made a novena and walked down the aisle.

"Just so Billy Galloway could twist her forever out of shape," is how my mother summed it up.

And I suppose there was some truth to all that. Even at eleven, I could see that this woman was no longer Lucia, the child bride of our picture album, glowing with the power of prayer. The woman in our livingroom that day was a disordered fifty-two-year-old who hid ten-dollar bills in the pages of her prayer book. There were tears in her eyes when she told my mother, "I just can't take anymore, Eleanor."

"You expected me to take it," my mother said. "My whole life in that house, you expected me to take it."

I'd heard that, too: the weeks on end when Billy lurked around, drunk and explosive, losing job after job, earning no pay.

"It's worse than ever," my grandmother said. "He's been drinking since the Fourth of July with no let up."

I imagined him with beer cans in both fists, the sky behind him aburst with colored firecrackers. I knew she was talking about a long time; this day was Valentine's Day. If it hadn't been for the snow, we would have exchanged cards that afternoon at school. All week long, we'd been slipping our envelopes into the red foil box which sat next to my teacher's desk.

"I was afraid I'd never see the end of it this time," my grandmother said. "Who else do I have to turn to?"

My mother, now silent, stared out our picture window toward the base, wishing, I suspected, for a tour of duty herself.

When she and Nan finally hoisted the bags and rounded the corner to the stairs, they bumped into me and Midget, huddled there against the wall. My grandmother put a hand on my mother's arm and spoke first.

"He's not a bad man, Rachael," she said.

My mother stiffened. "Mother, stop," she warned.

"I know what's said in this house, Eleanor," my grandmother said. "But it's because of the sickness, Rachael. Your grandfather can't help what he does."

"Don't you dare tell her that," my mother snapped. "And don't you ever pity a man, Rachael, I won't have it." Then she let the bags in her hands fall and stalked off, while my grandmother hauled her own baggage up to my room at the top of the stairs, where she was to share my small closet and double bed.

Looking back, I know my mother should've had Midget move in with me instead, should've given the small front bedroom to my grandmother. But my mother's fury prevented her giving my grandmother a place to call her own. Added to that, I suspect, was her determination to show me first hand what becomes of a woman with too soft a heart. I guess this worked, at first, when I was confronted with this old woman's possessions thrown around a room that used to be mine, when her heaving body next to mine every night felt so big and desperate that there seemed to be no space or air for me. I lay awake most nights, just to be sure I could keep on breathing. I saw Nan as the only one to blame, and I did, in the beginning, which made me fervently hate her.

To make things worse, I discovered that, when she thought I was already asleep, my grandmother would undress in my room, rather than using the bathroom in the hall. I hated this because I couldn't stop myself at those times from looking at her body, which swung every which way with too much flesh, so much extra flesh that she looked like a soft, white rhinoceros. Her brassiere hung to her stomach, each overflowing cup big enough to put my head in. I tried to tell myself that this was my own grandmother, but it didn't stop me feeling sick. It couldn't stop me, either, from staring down at my own chest and the small points which were starting to show there, wondering what kind of mistakes might doom me to have long, loose sacks of skin hanging in front of me, the way this grandmother did, wondering if I'd made some of those mistakes already.

And then there were mornings when I'd climb out of bed and see her, already outside in the red dawn, freshening the water of the bird bath or pouring seed into the feeders. I never believed that she was caring for the birds. I suspected that she had finished some ritual, and was hiding it by these actions. Full of distrust, I would meet her in the kitchen, and see her warming her hands over the gas flame.

"Don't tell your mother I was out there, Rachael," she'd wink. "She'd think I was wasting time and compassion."

Being only twelve, I had only begun to realize that, to my mother, all compassion was wasted. But I must have seemed just like her in those times, because I would merely shrug at this lady, believing as I did that she had something else up her sleeve, and feeling the need to hold on to my suspicions. There were depths of fury inside me that felt strange and powerful; keeping them to myself gave my life a mysterious secrecy that felt like womanhood. I thought those feelings meant more than the sight of my grandmother's breath streaking the sunrise. But I was wrong; because even now, the memory of her standing like an aged enchantress at the center of our barren yard makes my heart writhe inside of me.

A MONTH OR SO after my grandmother's arrival, I came home from school and saw an old battered pick-up sitting in our drive. It was green somewhere beneath all the dirt and rust, and had large letters hand-painted on the side which said "Galloway Plastering." Its sides were covered with spatters of hardened cement and the back was filled with ladders and tools and large pieces of fabric that looked like oily blankets. I looked at the truck for a long time, feeling ashamed that it was parked in front of our house, and feeling afraid to go inside. I sat my schoolbag down on the soggy ground next to a stick-bare forsythia, and wandered around the side yard where the ground was filled with stones, darkened and crunchy underfoot. I leaned against the gate, and my weight shook the fence which was rotting out of the ground. I looked off into the distance, and not over my shoulder at the truck. That was the year I liked best to pretend that all of the land, as far as I could see in all directions, was mine, and that the horizon was dotted with handsome cowboys who were all in love with me, even though I was their boss. I was, I'm sure, imagining this real well when I heard a clacking sound and saw Midget rolling around the side of the house in her old metal firetruck, pedaling and bumping along the uneven walk. Her hat had slipped off to the back of her head and the tie was caught in her coat zipper. Her face was white from cold and her nose was running. She wore only one mitten, and her other tiny hand was chapped and red.

"Come here, Midgy," I said, "your hat's off."

"I'm a fireman. The fire melted my head," she said, still busy pedaling over the broken sidewalk.

I knelt down and tucked her thin brown hair inside the hat, trying to straighten her up a little.

"I need the potty, Rachael, but mommy keeps hollering at the man and won't come to the door." She sniffed a little, and I used an old, hard tissue from my coat pocket to wipe her nose.

"That's Pop-pop Billy," I whispered.

"Well I have to go anyway," Midget said.

I helped her out of the firetruck and led her into the back door, to a small basement bathroom next to the washing machine. We could hear them yelling at each other in the kitchen upstairs, my mother's voice rising higher than her father's, neither one of them stopping to listen to the other.

"I raised you, Eleanor Jean," I heard him yelling.

"You couldn't raise your own ass off a bar stool," she yelled back. "I want you out of my house."

I wasn't about to climb the steps into that kitchen, so I led Midgy out into the back again, around to the side yard where I retrieved my schoolbag. Then we went to the front door and quietly let ourselves in, sneaking through the living room and up the front stairs to our bedrooms without being noticed. Midget promised to play quietly in her room, and I went to mine to do my homework.

As I walked into my room, I was startled to see my grandmother lying in bed, rather than being downstairs. And, she was not even lying across the bed with her clothes on, the way she usually did. She was under the blankets in a nightgown and robe.

"I just can't get up, Rachael," she said. "Don't let me bother your homework."

"But Billy is here," I said. "Your husband."

"I know, honey," she said. "It's best if I don't see him. Your mother can always handle him better than I can."

"Can she make him take that truck away?"

My grandmother smiled weakly. "I hope she can send him and his truck back to Florida before dinner."

That sounded right. I'd grown up believing that my mother knew how to get her way in most things, no matter what it took. So I figured she'd handle Billy, and get rid of him before dinner, just like Nan said she would. A whole new level of concern opened for me that day when I learned that my mother, even at her most powerfully mean, still couldn't face down the stuff of which Billy Galloway was made.

"Ain't nothin' in this green world can make me walk out that door without Lucia," he barked, setting up camp in our livingroom, yanking the recliner to the center of the room and slamming himself into it. From there, he bellowed what he had to say to my mother, who was slamming things in the kitchen, powerless.

"I'll *storm* that second floor of yours if I have to," he hollered.

I crept along the hallway to Midgy's door, and slipped into her room. Her coat and hat lay on the floor, but she was not in sight.

"You wanna stop me, Eleanor?" my grandfather's voice boomed again.

"I'll break your drunken legs," my mom screamed from the kitchen.

"Midgy?" I called, softly. A rustling came from beneath the bed. I knelt down and lifted the blanket. In the darkness, I saw the outline of my sister's face.

"I don't want the man to come up here, Rachael," she said, sniffling.

"He won't," I said. "I promise." I left her there and quietly went to the top of the stairs.

My grandfather was slouched in the chair, gripping the arms as if he were moving.

"Break my legs!" he was yelling, over and over. "I'd like to see you break my legs! I'd like to see you keep me from my own wife!"

I stood on the top step until he saw me. When he did, he straightened up and looked me in the eye.

"Who the hell are you?" he said.

"She doesn't want to see you," I said.

"Who doesn't?" he snapped at me, rising up from the seat.

I wanted to run, but locked my knees instead. "Lucia," I answered. "That's why she won't come down."

He fell back onto the seat of the chair, as if I'd shoved him. My mother, hearing my voice, came out of the kitchen with a look of disbelief on her face.

"Awright," Billy said. "If that's so, that's all I have to know. For now. But I won't go until I see her. She'll let me see her when she's ready."

Saying that, he breathed out all the air that was in him, collapsing back even farther onto the chair, turning his face away.

My mother continued to stare at me, her mouth open, her chapped hands twisting and untwisting a dishtowel, as if she were snapping the head off a chicken.

So LIFE IN OUR HOUSE was upended in a way it never was before. Billy sat, day after day, at the foot of our stairs, watching and waiting for word from above. He slept that first night on the couch in the livingroom. Then my mother got it into her head that he would ruin the fabric, so she hauled out a folding cot for the diningroom. He was refused a place at the family table, my mother telling him to his face that he could starve to death in her house for all she cared. I don't think he ate anything for several days.

Nan, day after day, refused to leave the bedroom. She knew well enough that, once under Billy's influence, she always did just about anything he wanted her to do. For the first time in her life, she had determined that she wasn't going to be overcome, and the only way she knew to prevent it was to place herself in hiding, to let her daughter, or anybody else who was willing, stand out in front and do the protecting. She no longer ate at the family table, either, so my mother placed me in charge of bringing a food tray up to her. During that time, I became her only contact with the outside world, since my mother did her best to avoid both parents completely.

As for my mother, she spoke to no one, not even me or Midgy. She moved in a silent rage that dared us to need her mothering. And when we couldn't help ourselves, she used up as much of the anger she could get out in whatever act of care was required. As she yanked my hair into a ponytail, or stuffed a poorly-made sandwich into a used lunchbag, I found myself wishing my father was not in the war. I liked to imagine that his presence would have changed the situation we were in. But the truth was that he wanted to be in Southeast Asia more than he wanted to be here. He chose sleeping in the mud, eating in mess tents, spending years at a time away from us all, leaving my sister and me to struggle as our mother was coming unglued.

One morning I entered the kitchen to find my mother staring into a bowl, watching the crumbling remains of a box of cornflakes, as they soaked up the orange juice she had mistakenly poured onto them. There was no other breakfast, and nothing for her to do but eat them, so she did, sitting across the counter from me, crying.

"What choice do I have?" she said out loud. "What choice do I ever have?"—sobbing and spooning mouthfuls of the ruined food past her lips. I knew just by looking at her that, if she had someplace else to go, she would have gone there. What I wasn't sure of then, and still wonder over now, is whether or not she would have thought to take her children. It was clear to me that, even before this invaded time, she saw Midgy and me as intruders, too; marauders of a different sort, who sucked her dry and hungered for more than she had to spare. Her world was a place where there was never enough time or patience or love to go around, not even for us; but I'm not sure if she ever saw that herself.

On this morning, she just kept spooning those flakes into her mouth, as if her vengeance would fix something. Then she sat with her eyes narrowed, muttering to herself, "There's more to this. There has to be. There's something she's not telling us," looking around our kitchen as if she'd find the answer sitting right out in the open. And this would have been true if she had once glanced at me. It was one of those moments when I was grateful that my mother never paid close attention to me, because those narrowed eyes and tight lips made her look capable of ferreting out any secret I ever held in my life. And by now my grandmother had sworn me to her own secret, which was that she had a lump the size of a ping-pong ball showing under the skin of her right breast.

I yelled out the night that I saw it, and Nan covered herself too late, looking at me with an expression somewhere between fright and anger. I thought I was going to be punished, but then her face softened, and she sat on the edge of the bed, draping her robe around her. She held out her hand to me, and I reluctantly took it.

"You have to promise you won't say anything about this," her other hand tightened around the robe. "It's a private thing," she said. "As private as your own most private thoughts and feelings."

I avoided her eyes, ashamed of the secrets I held, afraid that she knew my private thoughts and feelings.

"Rachael, I just want to make my own decisions for once. Can you understand that?"

I nodded, lying.

"Well, your grandfather doesn't," she said.

I nodded again because that's what she wanted me to do, but I kept watching her for some sign that would help me understand what she was asking of me. She continued to look me in the face, and slowly opened the robe, revealing her body from the waist up.

"Look at me, Rachael," she said. "Look what was done to me. No one is supposed to look like this."

Her breasts were bare. I stared at the way they hung, long and loose, with the nipples pointing down to the floor. The lump bulged beside one of the nipples, looking as though it would burst the skin. I didn't want to look.

"Mom says these things happen to all women," I said. "I'm getting some, too."

"Oh, honey," she said, hugging me to her. "Your mother doesn't understand. She doesn't know that your grandmother's body isn't normal. You will never look like this."

That's when she began to speak of an orphanage, out in the Delta swampland of Louisiana, of the nuns who bound the breasts of the girls to prevent their growth. These nuns checked their binding daily before Morning Prayer.

"They said it would keep us pure," my grandmother said. "But it hurt us. It hurt so much that we couldn't breathe. But there was no crying about it allowed. Crying caused us to be given penance."

I know I should have felt pity for her, but I was flooded with relief, knowing now that I would not grow loose flapping bags on my chest, as I had lain awake in fear of on so many of these nights.

"I had no power then, Rachael. I couldn't stop them from touching me. But I can now, and I will. For the first time in my life, I'm going to protect myself."

A look of determination sharpened her features. I sensed in her again that ability to withstand, to root herself like a tree in the soil of her conviction.

"If you tell anyone, they'll take me to a hospital. The doctors will cut into my body. I can't let anyone mutilate me again. God will understand."

I promised to keep silent. But I had no idea that the secret I was keeping for my grandmother was that she had decided to embrace the coming of her own death. I didn't know that there were several smaller lumps, or that this decision had everything to do with her need to lie down so frequently in the daytime. It was also the cause of the slight yellow tint that bewildered me when I looked at her skin in the sunlight. She would glow almost golden when she sat near the sun-filled window of my bedroom, watching the birds eat from the feeder she'd hung in a tree below the window. At times, now, she asked me to fill it, because she was too ill to venture out, even into the tender warmth of early April. I would do this reluctantly, not realizing the weakness of this failing woman, believing instead that she was forcing on me some secret knowledge of nature I had never felt a desire for.

ONE DAY AS SHE was eating from the tray I brought, my grandmother asked, "How does your grandfather look?"

"Like his truck," I said.

He did. He was not drinking in our house, but he had the battered, unkept look of a drunk. His blotched face was puffy, and his eyes were bloodshot and red-rimmed. His thin gray hair was greasy and uncombed. He wore the same wrinkled gray trousers and dirty green plaid flannel shirt each day. His sneakers and socks were marked and discolored. His coat was brown, worn corduroy with a mangy fake fur collar. Everything needed washing badly, but couldn't be washed because he had nothing else to put on his body. He slept in these clothes, not taking anything off all the days he was there, because he didn't pack anything else to put on.

When I relayed this to my grandmother, her eyes filled with tears. "Tell that mother of yours to have some pity for the man," she said.

"You tell her," I said.

My grandmother hung her head. "Please don't treat him like an animal, Rachael," she said. "He suffers more than anyone knows."

That someone could shed tears for this man confused me deeply. I felt afraid as I listened to him move through the house at night, hearing each of his moves in the kitchen, opening the refrigerator door—the silverware clanging just a little against a dish, the quick whistle of the teakettle snapped off. I kept the knowledge of his prowling to myself and did nothing for a while; then I told Nan.

"I want you to save him some food, Rachael," she said, as if it were a simple thing. "Anything will do."

She seemed unaware that what she asked was nothing short of treason. I didn't want to think about my fate should my mother catch me at such a thing.

"I can't do that," I said.

Nan looked at me, surprised. "There is no one else who can, dear"—as if that closed the subject and I had no choice.

So, I said nothing more, and began abetting the enemy that very night, dividing the leftovers into two separate bowls and hiding one way in the back of the lowest shelf of the refrigerator, where my mother wouldn't find it.

That night, I felt even more frightened when I heard him moving around, because I knew I had to go down into that darkness and stand before him. As my grandmother slept, I slipped from the bed and tiptoed down the hall. The silence that came from my mother's room rang with danger, and my heart burned in my chest. My nightgown clung around my legs as I inched down the stairs; moving slowly in the dark, I felt my way past the livingroom and diningroom furniture, following the dim light that glowed low beneath the kitchen door.

He was bent over a cup of coffee at the counter, looking out the window into the darkness, and he turned roughly when he saw me. "You want something?" he growled.

The cold of the linoleum was traveling into my feet and up my legs; I felt goosebumps rise on my skin as I tried to speak to him.

"I saved something for you," I said, going to the refrigerator and offering him the green plastic bowl of cold ravioli and meatballs.

"Who said I wanted this?" he asked gruffly, not looking inside.

"Nan said I should," I said.

Upon hearing that, he tore open the bowl quickly and sat at the table with a fork, eating the food right out of the plastic container. I sank into a chair and pulled my knees to my chin. With my arms wrapped tight around my legs, I could control my shaking. His hands were the first thing that caught my attention: they were big and wrinkled, with plaster in the creases. His nails were bitten down almost to the cuticles, so that the bulbous skin that's meant to be beneath the nail swelled up and over the tiny slivers. He never once looked at me. He lifted whole meatballs on the fork and ate them like ice cream scoops, biting around and around them until they were gone. Then he scooped up the ravioli and wolfed each of them down in one bite. He seemed anthropomorphic, newly emerged from the bowels of the earth, approximating as best he could the traits of man. His clothing was decorated with stains. His movements were wide and wild. Stuffing his food, slurping his coffee, moving with abruptness and great strength, he was nothing like my own father, for whom everything had a great deliberateness, an inflexible intentionality. Sitting beside Billy became a nightly experience of discovery— a plunge into wild places I wanted him to lead me through. I risked my mother's rage, gave up my own food, saved things for Billy from my own dinner plate. I felt enraptured by hunger and deceit, slept in class to stay awake with him. A new thrill—the thrill of not counting the cost—transformed everything I'd been raised to believe; all my mother's indoctrination about the misery of love, the avoidance of suffering, was melting away. Billy Galloway was everything to me.

"NAN SAYS NOBODY BELIEVES you love her," I said one night.

To my surprise, his eyes filled with tears. "I don't give a damn," he said, "I love that woman more than anybody'll ever understand. So what if I can't show it right?"

"But she's better here, for now, isn't she?"

He glanced at me and frowned. "Better how? I'm her husband."

"But we have heat," I said. "She gets lots of food. She gets to sleep as much as she needs to." He looked up sharply. "What do you mean as much as she needs to? Is she sleeping a lot? When is she sleeping?"

I sensed too late that I had slipped somehow, and tried to fix it. "She only sleeps some of the time," I said.

"In the day?"

"Not too much."

"How much?" he persisted.

"I don't know. I'm in school."

"Rachael, I think you're not saying what you know," he said.

"I'm not saying any more," I said.

He paused and looked at me, searching my face. "Does your mother know?"

I shrugged, "She never wants to know anything."

"Then don't tell her."

I looked at him. "It's Nan's secret. Not yours. I already promised her. I don't need to promise again."

He looked down at the table, and moved the cup away from the edge. He spread his hands out so that his gnawed fingers were splayed against the Formica. He spoke without looking at me.

"Promise me something else, then, and I will go away." He scribbled a telephone number on a napkin. "Call this number when the time comes, and ask for Ned. Tell him I'm your grandfather, and I need to get back."

I nodded, not knowing what time he thought was coming, looking at the napkin number. My grandfather studied my face. "You'll do this for me, Rachael?"

I nodded again, feeling the rise of panic at the thought of him going away. At the thought of returning to those nights, lying beside the body of my grandmother, sleepless with worry about nightmares and suffocation.

The next morning I did as my grandfather had asked and told Nan that he was leaving, saying he wanted just to talk to her before he went. She sent me downstairs right away to bring him up, and my mother intercepted us.

"Where do you think you're going?"

"I'm going to speak with my wife, Ellie," my grandfather said.

"Over my dead body," my mother said.

My grandmother opened the bedroom door. "Eleanor, I want to talk with my husband, if you please. Rachael can come in, too."

My mother was dumbfounded. "Rachael? What about me?"

"You don't understand what there is between your father and me," Nan said. "It's not your place to be here."

"I'M between my father and you," my mother bellowed, "because that's where you always put me!"

"Ellie, I'd rather you wait downstairs," my grandmother said. She allowed my grandfather and me to enter the bedroom, then she closed the door on my mother, who remained in the hall, too dumbfounded to speak again.

Billy took a few steps into the room, then stood awkwardly looking at his wife. My grandmother had dressed for the first time in weeks, and was wearing a flowered dress and blue glass beads.

"I know it's getting worse, Lucia," he said. "I know you've chosen for it to happen here."

"You gave me no choice, Billy," she said, "leaving me every night and day. I didn't want to die alone."

"Die?" I whispered, stunned. A glance at Billy told me he knew already.

"I'd never do that to you," he said, wringing his hat in his hands.

"You were doing it already, Billy," she said. Then, more gently, she added, "I know you don't know any other way."

His cheeks glistened with tears. "But can you forgive it?" he choked.

"When in my life, Billy Galloway, have I ever been able to do anything else?" my grandmother said.

"Then, let me hold you one last time, Lucia, and God forgive us both," he cried, folding her in his arms and rocking her gently with the force of the sobs he held inside.

I wonder: Did either of them once consider how I'd survive as their witness? As they revealed this bond which transports even the most damaged among us to a kind of heaven, did they hope I'd mistake it for love?

MY GRANDFATHER KEPT HIS WORD and left that day, even though I begged him not to. "It's all I can do now," he said.

"But she's *dying*," I said. "You have to stay."

He shook his head, looking off into the distance.

"I'm frightened," I said.

He looked back at me, sternly. "Hey now," he said. "You're stronger than that. You have an important promise to keep."

And he left me there, before I could renege. He left, and I was alone again, to face the rage of my mother, who now listed me among the enemy. How could I explain wanting to sleep with Midgy to a woman who refused to speak to me? So I kept a silent watch each night beside the body of my grandmother, terrified with each ragged breath, each moan, that this would be the time of her dying.

THE TIME DID COME, a few weeks later. It came with a shaking that rocked the bed and lifted Nan's wasted body again and again off the mattress. The convulsing hurled her into the air over and over as I tried, at first, to hold her down, not realizing that I uttered cries which pierced the dark and brought my mother charging into the room.

"What's the matter with her?" she screamed at me. "What are you doing?"

"I don't know," I cried. "I don't know what to do."

"You lying little bastard," my mother screamed, shoving me off the bed. "Get out of here you little son of a bitch."

I ran out of the room and down into the living room, to a corner behind the recliner, where I sank to the rug and stayed.

It was from that corner that I watched the doctors arrive and leave, from behind that chair that I heard the word "coma," and knew they saw great negligence in my mother's late attention to this matter. The older of the two doctors shook his head. incredulous.

"You've waited so long, Mrs. Meade, that it's not even worth making up a hospital bed. I don't give that woman twenty-four hours."

"No one told me she was sick," my mother said.

"By the looks of her skin, I'd say she's been jaundiced for months. Wouldn't that be a clue?"

I huddled even deeper in the corner, hearing the tone that this doctor used on my mother, knowing that somehow soon, the blame for all of this was going to land where it always did, right square on me. Midgy had curled up beside me, still in her sleepers, and I hugged her to me, rocking slowly, worrying about what would happen to me when this was all over. That's pretty much the way we spent the day, with the doctors seeing themselves out, my mother making up for lost time by raging at her unconscious, dying mother. Only once did Midget run into the kitchen to bring back a box of Kix for us to eat. And only once, after Midgy had been sleeping on the chair for hours, did I sneak over to the end table telephone, to call Billy's number at the Marina Bar. I said his wife would not wake up, and that he had to come.

Early the next morning, Billy returned, scrubbed and freshly dressed. A suit hung carefully on a hook in the back seat of a borrowed car. I answered his knock, and he entered the house, walking with me through the bedroom door, directly to his wife's side.

My mother stood quickly. "Get out of this room," she said, with eyes that darted hatred at me, promising me that, when this was all over, no torture would be overlooked.

"My wife wants me here," Billy said, moving closer to her body.

"Bullshit," my mother hissed.

That was when my grandmother lifted her wasted hand. We all watched it rise—so slowly it seemed to be moving through mercury—until it found the old fingers of her husband. He clutched at it quickly, enfolding her fingers softly.

"I'm here, Lucia," he whispered.

"Hypocrite," my mother spit.

Still, he remained there, as the rattle of his wife's breath grew weaker and the pause between the lift and fall of her chest grew longer, holding her hand and never once letting it drop until it was clear to everyone in the room that she wouldn't breathe again.

His right and authority went unchallenged when he finally looked up and said, "Well. I guess this is how it ends. I guess this is how she meant to go."

Then he excused us all and waited alone with his wife. My mother stormed away, but I lingered outside the door close enough to hear his voice, soft and gentle, as he whispered to her things that no one else was meant to hear. When the mortician arrived my grandfather helped him slide the body into the long, zippered bag, directing him sternly to take great care, guarding her as he and I both knew she would have wanted to be guarded. The last I saw of him that day, he had climbed into the back of the black limousine, and as the car edged slowly down the driveway, he held his wife's covered body against himself, doing his best to cushion her from the bumps of the road.

My mother watched him out the same window, her jaw set and angry.

"It's a little late to love her now, you bastard," she hissed. "Since you're the reason she's dead."

ON THE DAY of the funeral, I woke early and was startled to see a figure red with the sunrise standing in the center of our yard. I hurriedly tiptoed down to the back and out into the dissolving darkness. My grandfather turned when he felt me approach.

"This was her spot, wasn't it?" he asked.

I nodded.

He smiled down at me sadly. "She was a special one," he said.

Shyly, I slid closer to him, gratified at how quickly he closed his roughened fingers around my chilled shoulder.

He looked down at me. "I'll be goin' away now, you know. I'm sure nobody in there's gonna mind it," he indicated with his head toward the house.

It hadn't yet occurred to me that Billy wasn't going to stay, that he wouldn't stay for me. I hadn't yet realized that these were my last moments of safety.

"I'll go, too," I said.

He removed his hand from my shoulder and nodded his head slowly. "That you will, someday," he said, "and it will be a distance."

He spoke the words easily, as if the torn fabric of my life could be tacked together by a simple pronouncement, as if the certainty of my mother's uncontrollable fury was no concern of his.

I wrapped my arms tightly around my chest, where it felt, all of a sudden, as if something big had cracked.

"This is why my mother hates you," I said, realizing the edges of something too vast to see all at once.

Billy's face stayed empty. The blue of his eyes was too diluted, too watery; I saw no reflection of myself in them.

"They're throwing the only one who ever cared about me in a fresh-dug hole today," he said. "The rest of you can all go to hell, the whole stinkin' lot of you."

I tried to answer, but my throat closed and my lips wouldn't move. When he walked away, I couldn't do anything but watch, having lost all feeling of connection to my body. I felt too small to be seen by human eyes, and too far away from everything human, even my own human self, to even be real.

I knew I shouldn't have expected more, and probably didn't, not deep down where I kept my real truths about people. Maybe I just wanted to forget it for a while. But when Billy walked away from me, I swear, the cracking in my chest hurt so bad I'd have prayed out loud for a real mother, if I thought anything of praying. I wouldn't have asked God for much, either: just for somebody true who'd stay, who'd always come and hold me. Somebody who'd, maybe, smooth my hair, or rock me if I let it go and cried. I wanted so bad to feel somebody's warm whisper against my cheek, saying, "Ssh. It's all okay." And to whatever words I'd let pour from inside me, they'd only need to nod nicely and tell me, "I know, honey. I know."

Red

LAST PERIOD FRIDAY at Irwin Middle School: Chairs banging against desks, and thump-clanging school bags and metal lunch boxes sounded like a wagon train pulling free of a fast-burning town. The Ancient History teacher stood, her hand on the knob of the classroom door, right beneath the metal-framed photo of President Lyndon B. Johnson.

"Y'all need to spend some time this weekend studying your Egypt facts," she called over the din.

Miss Elwood lived off-post all by herself, far down a dirt road outside Rayford, with three Rocky Mountain goats and a pen full of red-eyed white rabbits her only company. She had pictures of her animals on her desk, the way some people have pictures of their families, and each one of the creatures had a human name. The kids thought those animals at one time might have been annoying students she hexed. But Midgy Meade, who was still struggling to buckle her schoolbag there at the back of the line, felt a sad familiarity in Miss Elwood, a sorrowful gentleness that moved between them like a whispered secret Midgy would someday be able to hear.

"We're having the test Monday, right after class bell, no shilly-shallyin'," Miss Elwood finished up saying.

A frightful fluttering in her heart shook Midgy right down into her stomach and that's when she decided she couldn't show up for school on Monday. It was the first important test she'd have to take since her big sister Rachael went away the month before, skipping her senior year at Cape Fear High with a scholarship for college in New Orleans. Rachael always helped her study, and helped her straighten out the words when they got all jumbled on her worksheets. It was a secret between them that they kept from their mother, because with their dad still in Vietnam, their mom cried every day. They figured she didn't need any more trouble than what the TV and newspapers brought into their lives. And it wasn't like Midgy was giving up too easily, either. But middle school was a lot harder than Bowley Elementary, with more reading and writing and more teachers demanding that she work faster than she was able. Midgy tried her hardest to memorize the Egypt dates and places all on her own because Miss Elwood called Egypt a vast and important Empire. She said they generously offered their influence to other more backwards people. And when those people refused to appreciate it, Miss Elwood said the wise Egyptian leaders had no choice but to conquer them for their own good. So Midgy tried hard to study, but all those numbers and letters just got mixed up in front of her eyes, turning backwards and jumping around on the page. Hatshepsut, Thutmose III, Tutankhamen. They weren't names like any people she knew in their part of North Carolina and she imagined Miss Elwood's red marks all over her test paper, a big red "F" at the top. Even with all her studying, the only words Midgy could ever remember were Delta, which is where her own family came from, and Memphis, which was where Elvis the King now lived in a Palace. That much she knew, and she wondered if Egypt had been around them somewhere, long ago, like sometime before the Korean War. Otherwise, why'd they have to learn it?

But when she mentioned that idea to her friend Tommy on their way back to the Normandy Units, he only laughed.

"Korea was when your sister was born," he said. "Do you think it was Egypt here then?"

"I guess she would have mentioned it," Midget said. She thought about it a little more as they walked, neither of them saying too much for a while. "Then maybe it was before Korea, like when your father was born," Midget finally said.

Tommy looked at her with his angriest expression. It was the face he had where his lips got tight and nearly disappeared and where his breathing sounded like a growling in his throat.

"You know I never had no father," he said. "How the hell do I know if it was Egypt then?"

"I meant the Robarts," Midgy said.

"Fosters ain't parents," Tommy said.

They walked awhile more without talking. She and Tommy had been best friends even in diapers, so she knew well enough that whenever Tommy got mad at her he'd just take some time and come back around. A few jeeps filled with young soldiers rumbled by. They shouted and saluted to Midgy as she straightened the beret on her head and saluted back. She watched as Tommy fought back a smile, and saw his shoulders begin to relax.

It wasn't an official beret she wore, but one she made in Home Ec last spring, when all the other girls were making flower-print mini-skirts. She pieced it together from remnants of green wool she dug from the sewing bin and then decorated it with patches like the ones her dad wore: the blue one with the yellow sword and three yellow thunderbolts, the green one with the two gold arrows crossed in an "X" and her favorite, the red one with the skeleton head, the airborne wings and anchor. She was so proud of that beret, she wore it straight through the summertime when the heat of the wool on her head left her hair dripping wet. If her dad could wear his over there in the jungles, she figured she could wear hers here at Bragg where it wasn't nearly so scorching as that.

"Well, maybe someday we can go to Memphis and check that Egypt stuff out for ourselves," Tommy said finally, his fingers scratching at his messy blond hair. "I hear Tennessee ain't too far."

"That'd be fine," she said slowly. "Except I think they got it all in museums now and there's nothing left on the streets."

They were standing in front of Midget's house. The sun was like golden cream, pouring through the leaves of the front yard sour gum tree. Midgy had been watching those leaves the last few days as they started their turning from green to red. She never could figure out how something could jump from one way of being right into another like that, and each year she tried to chart it out. But there was a suddenness to it that just happened on her, always coming like a shock. Some of those green leaves that she watched just this morning were hanging there now, red as blood could be.

"You still studying on them leaves?" Tommy asked her, watching her stare into the tree.

"Haven't figured it out yet, have I?" she said, bending her face deeper in, getting the branches tangled in the beret and the little waves of her chestnut hair that tumbled from beneath it.

Tommy suggested that they pull them off and watch them in the comfort of their homes.

"They gotta be attached," she said. "Otherwise the red never happens at all."

"Why not?"

"'Cause bein' attached is what keeps 'em alive," Midgy said, pulling her face back out of the tree branches, "least that's what I guess is why."

"Ain't that what turns 'em dead?" he asked.

Midgy shrugged, "That too, I guess."

"Well, she ain't never gonna let you have that camera, anyway," he said.

"I already took it. It's in my suitcase, under the bed."

Since it was only early October, she figured she had some time to keep watching, and could sneak her dad's old Argus outside each morning to take pictures day by day. That way, she hoped to watch the miracle happen in slow motion, shot by shot.

Her mother wouldn't notice. She was studying hard at the university and doing something that was a kind of secret about the War. It kept her tied up all the time with her best friend, Hedy Perco, who lived in the house attached to theirs with only her youngest son Pauly now left at home. Her husband and the older boy, Vince Jr. were both in Vietnam with Roy, Midgy's dad.

One night, her mom and Hedy had some people in for a meeting, and Eleanor warned Midgy not to tell.

"We gotta keep this between us," she said, "Because if anybody on post finds out, we'll get kicked out of our housin' for sure."

It had something to do with telling boys to turn in their cards, that much Midgy knew. At first she thought it was "cars," but found out it had something to do with papers that come to your door telling you to go to the war. It was something they were doing up north in big cities, and her mom was helping in secret on campus right here near the post. Midgy didn't understand why her mother told people not to go, especially since she cried so much with worry about her dad. Wouldn't she want them there to help him, she wondered, instead of leaving him all alone? But Midgy just nodded and promised her mom and then kept raising the flag in their backyard every morning, like her daddy showed her how to the last time he was home. She was only in the fourth grade then and felt really proud that he taught her and trusted her with something he said was so important. She felt that doing it just right every day would keep them all safe somehow, like a kind of American magic.

INSIDE THE HOUSE, Eleanor stood holding a mug of instant coffee, watching her daughter outside on her front law with that ragamuffin Tommy Buonorotti. He was one of the fosters that the Robarts took in, a scraggly kid whose clothes never fit him right. Tommy Bones, the kids called him, because you could count his ribs right through whatever hand-me-down shirt was hanging on him. Still, he wasn't a bad kid, and Eleanor had to acknowledge to herself that she liked the way he seemed so attentive to Midgy. The two of them had some kind of bond from the time they were toddlers at the playground. And they were a raggedy pair, Eleanor had to admit, with Midgy being something of a tomboy with that short-cropped haircut and those beat-up Levis she insisted on wearing tucked into her cowboy boots like the men on post who'd passed jump training. And she'd had a habit since she was just a toddler of pulling her hair out while sucking her thumb which she never grew all the way out of it. She didn't suck her thumb anymore, as far as Eleanor knew, but she still twisted her hair when she got nervous. Eleanor thought Tommy's devotion to her daughter was sweet, all things considered.

The only person she had that kind of bond with was Hedy Perco, her best friend since they both came to Bragg in '56. From the time Eleanor met her, Hedy seemed stuck like some caged exotic bird, unhappily married and trapped there in the Normandy Units. When their husbands were sent off to Southeast Asia that year as part of a Special Forces operational detachment, it was Hedy who cared enough about Eleanor's sorrow to take her on escape trips off post, to sit in a diner in downtown Fayetteville and drink ice cream sodas or go to the movies whenever a new film was released, like "High Society" or "The Ten Commandments." Eleanor smiled to think of that now: Hedy the tough-talking Pittsburgh runaway in her beatnik black stretch pants and tunic tops, her black ballet slippers and silver jewelry, her auburn hair spilling over her shoulders and Eleanor, the shy New Orleans child-bride in her silly poodle skirt and initial sweater, her dark hair in a ponytail wrapped in a nylon scarf. They were different as could be, but over time, they became the best of friends. With their husbands gone for years at a time, neither woman had more than a handful of consecutive months of marriage. So this friendship was the longest relationship either of them had. For a long time, Eleanor kept Roy's letters beneath the pillow on his side of the bed, believing it was like keeping his love there with her, protected and safe. But it didn't do her any good; and when there came a day when she let the dream die, it was only Hedy who knew why and consoled her. Hedy, for her part, never felt that kind of loyalty to Vince. In fact, she'd been taking those new pills and having boyfriends for a while now. She called it "putting on her red dress," and never made apologies. Her men were always from off-post and this time it was a poli-sci professor right there at Fayetteville State, a long-haired liberal named Jackson. They met at the campus bookstore, where Hedy and Eleanor worked part-time, which of course had been Hedy's idea. It was Eleanor's idea, though, to start taking some classes in journalism, since she always wanted to write. Hedy wanted no part of the classes, although she read everything on the shelves at the bookstore: Anthropology books, books on Educational Law, textbooks on Geology, or Calculus.

It was through Jackson that they both got involved in working against the war. He was part of the National Mobilization Committee, a coalition to fight involvement in Vietnam, and advised his students about draft resistance.

One night he took them to an off-campus bar and ordered a whole bottle of Echo Spring Bourbon. The three of them drank until it was nearly gone, talking politics and war.

"Protecting Democracy against the Reds is what they call it," he said. "But we're really protecting is Capitalist expansion. Saving the world for democracy means saving it for IBM, for Big Oil, for Wall Street and the Industrialists. That's why you've got to get involved."

Hedy and Eleanor looked at each other without answering.

"What?" Jackson said, "Am I wrong?"

"We're married to officers," Eleanor said. "How the hell can we be involved in what you're doin'?"

"*I'll* do it," Hedy said.

"What?" Eleanor nearly choked on her bourbon.

Hedy fixed her with a stare. "You have daughters, Ellie," she said. She looked as though she were about to cry, but choked it back. "Vince Jr.'s already there," she said. "Now Pauly's talking enlistment. Screw Jackson's liberal bullshit. It's my own flesh and blood on those missions."

Nearly six months ago, Eleanor watched Hedy put her oldest boy, a newly graduated Green Beret, on a transport plane bound for Saigon. Her daughter Rachael cried for a week about him going. There'd been something between them that Eleanor didn't want to think about, and she hoped that with Vince, Jr. gone and Rachael away at school, her daughter would gradually forget about the romance. She hoped Rachael could begin a new life far outside of Bragg and never know about a broken heart.

Eleanor understood why Hedy would counsel young boys. She knew it was her own sons' faces her friend saw when she looked at each and every one of them. So right there, over that table with the puddles of Echo Spring reflecting the crimson neon lights from behind the bar, over the floating empty peanut shells, Eleanor took her friend's arm.

"Okay," she said, "I'm in."

A little while later, on their way back to the post together, Hedy thanked her friend again. "Ellie, I lay awake at night, my whole body aching with fear. It feels like premonition, or clairvoyance. I smell blood, I taste death, I see myself cradling someone in my arms."

Eleanor nodded. "I bet every woman with sons imagines that they'll die," she said, trying to console her friend. "It's deep in our brains as Christian women don't you think? That image of Mary with her own dead Jesus?"

THERE WAS A CRAWLSPACE behind the wall of the downstairs family room, a tiny access door behind the couch. Midgy knew her mother stored their old toys in there, things she thought they'd need again someday—wagons, tricycles, a Shirley Temple doll wrapped in a soft blanket and stored in a big box.

The floor inside the crawlspace was rough-edged and dusty. But Midgy's mission was to fix it up in secret through the weekend, ever since she came home knowing about the test coming up on Monday. The access door was a small rounded opening, only big enough for Midgy to get through on her hands and knees. Inside, it was dark and damp. The air smelled dead and ancient, with no light coming from the outside world. So she snuck down her flashlight collection, making sure to fill them with fresh batteries from the drawer in the kitchen. She pulled an old, deflated raft from the outside shed and laid it near the crawlspace door. Then she blew it up for a bed. A blanket or two from the upstairs closet would make it just fine for sleeping, or for laying there and looking through some Millie the Model comic books.

She figured her teacher would make them label a map. There was always a darn map. She never could write things small enough, even when the letters didn't jumble themselves around. Besides, if she was sick, she knew Miss Elwood would let her come in the next day at lunch and talk the answers, like she did with the mythology quiz when Midgy actually threw up. And talking her answers was something she could do much better anytime.

The last thing she took down to the crawlspace was her shoebox of troll dolls, careful to leave a few around her bedroom, so her mom wouldn't notice them missing.

"You just shush now," she said to the ones she'd set up on her headboard. "You'll be the guards, standing here looking normal so that nothing calls attention to our plan of action."

The trickiest thing was the note she knew she had to write. She started working on it Sunday, figuring she'd leave it on the kitchen table in the morning so her mom wouldn't be suspicious of her being gone. She thought about it and decided to write:

I had to leave early to help Mr. Ferryman with the puppies.

Mr. Ferryman was the school custodian. Eleanor knew that the lost Irish Setter who lived on the school grounds just had a small litter, and that one of the male pups had already died. So this excuse was something Midgy knew her mom would believe. Midgy formed each letter carefully and slowly, hoping that, without Rachael to check, there wouldn't be anything backwards that she didn't find herself.

She didn't sleep well that night because her plan called for getting up very early and into the crawlspace before her mother woke up. Sometime around 0400 she figured would be a good idea. Besides, she was sleeping in her Levis not to waste time. They scratched against her legs and the zipper dug into her stomach as she tossed beneath her blankets, which made her stomach cramp.

The shadows through the house were very deep when she felt her way down the stairs and through the living room the next morning. In the kitchen, she had to depend on the tiny light that her mother had left burning, the one over the stove that acted as a kind of nightlight. She pulled the note she wrote out of her pocket and smoothed it out on the kitchen table. It looked pretty good. But she worried that her mom would come to her classroom with lunch. So she found a pencil on the counter and wrote:

P.S. Don't worry. I packed my own lunch.

And here she realized that she needed to leave evidence. So she made a peanut butter and strawberry preserves sandwich. Then she added marshmallow fluff, just because she liked it. She put the knives in the sink and wrapped the sandwich in Reynolds Wrap, liking how the silvery stiffness felt like something a soldier would use. She put it in a brown grocery bag, and because it looked very empty in there, she added oatmeal raisin cookies and an apple. Looking around at the kitchen, she decided to leave the peanut butter on the table. She splashed some cookie crumbs on the counter for good measure.

It wasn't until she was tiptoeing down the stairs to the den that she thought of the flag. Every morning, Midgy took the folded flag that sat on the washing machine overnight back outside to the flagpole. Slowly and carefully, she unfurled the fabric and hooked it back onto the pole. Then, she raised it, hand over hand, until the flag flew high above the roof of her home, flapping in the breeze or hanging limply in the still air. Just like she promised him, this had become Midgy's determination, to fly that flag for her daddy, as a way to signal him home. But it was four a.m. and the sun hadn't risen. The flag can never fly at night, her dad had told her. So she decided to wait and sneak out after Eleanor had gone, raising it then when the sun was finally up.

She kept on creeping down the stairs and moved behind the sofa to the little door which she pushed quietly, now that she was on her hands and knees, then climbed in and closed it carefully behind her.

She curled up on the raft and pulled the blankets over her. One flashlight was all she would allow herself, so that nothing would shine outside the door. Her plan had been to look through all the her comic books, one after another. She couldn't read them too well, so she made up stories that went with the pictures. But after a few pages of telling the stories to herself she fell asleep, one hand holding the flashlight handle, the other clutching her favorite issue, where Millie was modeling in New York City, and Midgy decided that the cute photographer, Clicker, had finally become her boyfriend.

W HEN THE ALARM WENT OFF at seven, Eleanor pulled the blankets up around her chin, not wanting to move out of bed. From the open bedroom window, she smelled autumn blowing in and felt weak against the coming of the chill. The flowers would be dying, then gone until next Spring. The air would carry that scent of cold bland pond water. It was a few weeks now since Rachael had gone away, and the feel of her presence in the house was fading. Every morning before waking Midgy for school, Eleanor would enter Rachael's bedroom where the air still smelled of patchouli incense. She'd look once again at the peace sign throw pillows, the Joni Mitchell poster, the Jefferson Airplane album leaning against the bookshelf. She would sit softly on the bed and lay her head on the pillow her daughter had slept on, breathing in the dark chocolate scent of her hair. She didn't wash the sheets on the bed, just smoothed and preserved them as they had been the last night her daughter slept wrapped in them before going away to New Orleans.

It's a gift, this intelligence of hers, people said. And maybe that was true. But Eleanor believed that Rachael had climbed into her own brain long ago and hid there, like someone barricading herself in the attic of a house she feared to live in. Eleanor closed her eyes and imagined her beautiful daughter walking shyly across the campus, her long dark hair making her look like a Choctaw princess as she moved gently, carrying all her beloved books.

"Just don't fall in love, Rachael," she whispered to the image. "Please don't."

She thought of Jackson again, and his political speeches. She thought of Roy and his covert missions. What do men know of life, Eleanor wondered, that makes them see things so differently? All around her at Bragg she saw women alone, holding up the world, raising up the children. It wasn't the life she meant for herself to have. But Eleanor's dreams for a real family life with Roy had died so long ago that she didn't even bother to mourn them anymore, and that wasn't something she could ever feel right about. At least Rachael was in a civilian world now, safe from military life. Eleanor hoped there would be no threat of a soldier son-in-law. No early widowhood. No hysterical phone calls at 4 a.m. when her daughter realized for the first time that her soldier husband was shacking up on the other side of the world with some caramel-colored Third World woman, the way Eleanor herself realized all those years ago. She stood slowly, and straightened the tie-dyed bedspread. "I love you sweetheart," she whispered, patting the pillow one last time before moving away.

Down the hall, Eleanor opened Midgy's bedroom door to tell her it was time to get up. But this room, too, was empty. Midgy's Barbie Doll bedspread had been pulled up across the bed and tucked unevenly beneath the pillows which lay in two lumps near the headboard. The troll dolls had been moved around, all facing the door like Imperial Watchmen. Their hair was blue or orange or yellow and stood straight up on their heads, pointing toward the ceiling. The dwarf-shaped bodies were naked and their little pot-bellies protruded like pregnant troll mothers. Their hard glass eyes stared with a kind of dead happiness at the door. The sight of them never failed to unnerve Eleanor. She closed the door quickly and moved toward the first floor, calling for her daughter.

DOWN BELOW, MIDGY WOKE to her mother's voice as it traveled closer. She never considered how it would feel to hold back her answer when her mother called. Something in her wanted to cry out, "I'm here! I'm here!" But she held herself still and heard Eleanor move into the kitchen. She imagined her mom. standing in her curlers, reading the note and seeing the clues Midgy left behind. Midgy began to smell perking coffee, and hear the song from the radio that her mother had turned on: "... *Johnny's in the basement mixing up the medicine, I'm on the pavement, thinking 'bout the government . . .*"

Her mom used to listen to a blonde lady named Doris Day. She listened to somebody named Andy Williams singing Hawaiian songs. Now she listened to the college radio station and studied how to write for newspapers. Midgy liked it. The thing Midgy loved the best was how her mom's hair had gone soft now. It was a shining black color and she threw away her hairspray, so it fell around her face like silk and moved easily in the wind. Midgy wished she had that hair instead of her short stubby hair which, she knew, was her very own fault. She still hadn't been able to stop pulling it out on that one side of her head, and the only way to keep her from getting a good grip was for her mother to keep it cut short like some girl called Twiggy that Rachael showed her in the beauty magazine, trying to make her feel better. There was still a little bald spot that Mimi the hairdresser had to work real hard to conceal. But the beret worked fine covering that.

It was for sure that her mom was different now, going to those meetings for continental objections, and Midgy even thought that Eleanor might say okay to her skipping the Egypt test. But she didn't want to take the chance of that. She figured she'd have to start with something else—something smaller that she'd have to think about, as a kind of science experiment. Besides, her mom still cried a lot. Midgy felt funny in her stomach, lying there in the dark, hearing her mom move through the house above her. It hurt with a deep ache, and Midgy wondered if she was doing something very wrong by burying herself away like this. She felt like she was lying with her whole body, while her mom sat upstairs sipping her coffee, trusting that her daughter was feeding puppies at the school. She closed her eyes and tried to sleep again, hoping that it would help to wash away this feeling of badness that had come over her. A heavy resentment of empires, dead rulers, tombs filled with crap and all the archeologists of the world filled her, and she blamed them for making her into a sneak and a liar. What good was all their power and war and conquering if they were all just dead now anyway? She felt clammy and shaky and pulled the blankets up to her shoulders, turning her face into the rubber hardness of the raft, and willed herself to sleep.

IT HAD BECOME a beautiful morning, and Eleanor drove the Impala to campus, its windows rolled open, the Rolling Stones' "Let's Spend the Night Together" playing on the radio. Sunlight blazed on the aquasilver paint of the car's hood, and Eleanor put her sunglasses on to deflect the dancing glare. Roy surprised her with the Chevy the last time he was home, raving about its V8 engine and dual-speed power glide, as if Eleanor had any idea what he was talking about. But it was nearly new and she liked the huge trunk and seat space, which was perfect when she and Hedy took the kids off post for picnics and long trips to the beach. Hedy's own car, a '64 convertible VW, cherry red, had no room at all; but she picked it out herself, driving it onto the post, honking and calling out for Eleanor to come see what she just bought. Eleanor had never picked out her own car, and was in awe of how easily Hedy made those kinds of decisions, never once thinking of asking Vince his opinion or permission. For her part, Eleanor tried never to think about Roy and the adoring girl he kept in Nha Trang, or how they probably rode together, holding hands, in the back of a cyclo pedaled by some bare-legged brown man. No. She tried her hardest to use the Impala as if her husband didn't give it to her out of guilt for the things he did on the other side of the world.

In her journalism class, they had worked on interviewing techniques, and she had typed up her interview assignment on the Regal the night before with almost no typing mistakes. She felt ready for her presentation that morning and almost good about herself today, for a change not minding so much about being an older student. She thought again of Rachael, who was closer to her classmates ages, and wondered how it would feel to be in class with her own daughter, which is the way she looked at the girls who sat around her in her studies. Then she thought of Hedy, who still acted like a 20-year-old herself sometimes, parading around in front of Pauly's friends, young enough to be her own children, wearing that faded black and white polka-dot bikini of hers. Just the idea of attracting boys' hormonal attention gave Eleanor the creeps. She had gone dead altogether in that area, and wanted no attention, no contact. There had been no lovers for her, ever. And now, with all her schoolwork piled on Roy's side of the bed and his letters packed in a box in the closet, she realized that what replaced him these days were the books and papers and notes of this new effort she had taken on. And that was what she decided to do for her interview: talking to Bragg wives about how they dealt with loneliness. She was surprised how openly they talked to her. Jeannne Baker, over in Anzio Acres, got to obsessing about the kind of lawn she grew, always thinking that Earl would care if she let the lawn go to seed. Mary Robart started taking in the foster kids, filling up her time with their childhood diseases. Others took up knitting, or church-going. A few began a reading circle. Several just developed those vacant kinds of stares that signaled an empty life tumbling out of control. And some of them talked about the new battery-powered substitutes they'd taken on, giggling about how the drawers of their night tables contained the only part of a man they really needed. She hoped her grade would be good, turning in such an honest field interview on the subject of Loneliness and The Fort Bragg Wife.

IT WAS NEARLY THREE when Midgy woke on the raft. She had slept badly and still felt queasy near her stomach. The Cinderella watch on her wrist had a slightly scratched face, but Midgy shined the flashlight directly on it and realized how late it was. She was rolling herself into a kind of stooped sitting position when she first felt a strange kind of wetness on the sides of her thighs. She felt with her hand and knew for sure that something was wrong. The flashlight she aimed at herself showed a kind of reddish brown stain on both sides of her jeans. She stared for a long time, not knowing what she was looking at. At first, she thought that her legs might be bleeding, but she sneaked out quietly into the den and through the laundry room door into the bathroom near the washing machine. It didn't take long for her to realize that the blood was in her underpants, too.

"This is really bad," she whispered, starting to cry.

So many things rushed through her head. She thought she was getting punished for her sneakiness and lying and the whole Egypt thing. She thought it was because of the flag, which still lay folded on top of the washing machine.

What if that flag flying was the only thing that kept her daddy safe, she worried. What if he was shot down and bleeding somewhere in the jungle and this was just a sign of it to let her know what she did?

She wondered if such a thing was possible, that people could be bleeding at the same time in some magical way, if this was a sign that somebody she loved was dead.

She did the best she could do to wipe her legs with the toilet paper, wetting it in the water from the laundry tub, and scrubbing the dried blood from her skin. Then she pulled herself back together and went to do the only thing that felt right; she called Tommy.

Luckily, it was already after school, and he answered the phone right away.

"Tommy, I'm dying," she said. "I need you to come with the doctors' kit."

Tommy's foster father had been a medic before he was killed in the war, and his old bag was left in his closet at the house, along with some of his other belongings. Tommy was always sneaking it out of the house so that they could perform whatever medical cures were necessary, mostly on the neighborhood dogs and cats. This was the first time they would be using it on a person.

He hurried right over, since they lived only a few doors apart, and came right into the laundry room door.

"How'd it happen?" he said.

"I don't know," she told him. "I just started bleeding there."

"Can't be true," he said, opening up the bag and pulling out some tools. "You must have bumped something. You fell, I bet."

"Never did, Tommy. All I been doing is hiding in the crawl-space."

"Well, then, that's it. Something from the crawlspace bit you."

"Nothing was in there."

"Invisible then. Just cause you don't see something doesn't mean it can't hurt you."

Midgy was watching him unload the bag: stethoscope, the funny ear light thing, tongue depressor Popsicle sticks.

"You bring Band-Aids?" she asked.

"You probably need stitches."

She put her hands on her hips. "OH NO," she said. "No-body's stitching me there. How would I pee?"

Tommy just stood looking at the bloody jeans.

"You better call Rachael," he said. "Maybe she'll come home and take you to the hospital. I'd do it but I'd have to drive the station wagon. The last time I did that Mrs. Robart called me a Bombing Nation and tried to ship me back to the foster home."

They placed a long-distance call to New Orleans, to the hall telephone in Rachael's dorm. It wasn't until she heard her sister's voice on the phone, sounding so good and making her feel so lonely, that Midgy began to cry.

"Tommy says I need stitches. I stole the Argus and I think I killed daddy," she finished up by saying.

"Oh, honey," Rachael said, "it has nothing to do with the crawlspace, or the flag, or Egypt. You didn't do anything wrong."

She told her that it had to do with biology, that her body had changed to a woman's body now.

"Well, where'd my old body go?" Midgy said.

"Nowhere, exactly. It's the same body, just becoming differ-ent because you're growing up."

"Is there some medicine I can take to stop it?" Midgy asked.

Midgy was thinking that she might bleed forever now.

"Mom never told you about this?" Rachael asked. "Don't any of your girlfriends have it?"

Midgy said she never knew one bit. She hated this idea. Who thought of such a stupid thing, anyway?

"It just happens, all of a sudden?" she asked.

"I never thought to tell you honey," Rachael said. "I'm sorry. You just seem so little to me, I guess." She told her where to go in her room to find some sanitary napkins.

"The school nurse might have some pamphlets on this," Rachael said.

"She smells like moth balls, Rachael," Midgy answered.

Rachael said she would try to come home the following weekend. She said that Midget had to tell their mom now.

"She's not home," Midgy said.

"Then go next door to Mrs. Perco," Rachael said, "she'll know."

ELEANOR'S CLASS WENT BADLY. Her professor told her to stop talking when she was only part of the way through her presentation.

"What makes you think that anyone would care, Mrs. Meade, about your topic?"

Eleanor's face burned and she found that she couldn't summon a voice to answer him. She stood paralyzed there in the front of the room as he strode toward her. She felt the other students' eyes on her and felt completely bare and humiliated.

"How do you imagine you will ever get your articles read when you are writing about something like "Loneliness and the Fort Bragg Wife'?"

Eleanor swallowed hard and finally spoke, her voice coming out as barely a whisper. "You said write your best about what you know and you'll find an audience," she said.

"Real Americans want nothing to do with you people at Bragg," he said, coldly. "Real America doesn't want what you people have made of the world. What you've made here in Fayettenam," he gestured around himself. "What do we give a damn about your 'loneliness'?"

Eleanor stood unsteadily, her legs shaking wildly, and clutched her work to her chest. Her first desire was to flee without a word, fearing that she would never win a battle against this man. But she had promised herself and worked her hardest to do this assignment well, and the unfairness of what the professor said began to blaze inside her. Hedy would fight back, she thought, and she tried to stand taller the way she knew her friend would.

"Dr. Lawler," she said. "Real America includes us women in them houses there at the post. We're real, too. And don't you think we're just as scared and sick at heart as everybody else?" She looked around the room at the young faces staring at her now, but saw no look of understanding. Somehow, her voice grew stronger anyway as she pointed to them. "I have a daughter your age away at college," she said. "Don't you think I'm glad she's outa here? Don't you think I pray every night to leave Bragg myself? To be away from what I got no control over? Why do y'all think I'm here learnin' to write about the truth?"

She turned again to Lawler, surprised by her readiness, now, to face him down. "I'm proud of what I wrote, and if you bothered to read it, you would see that it's good. It isn't perfect," she said. "But it's good. And it's honest. And somebody should read it."

Lawler continued to stare at her coldly. "Well it won't be read by me," he said. Slowly he extended his arm toward her, and flicked his fingers at her dismissively. "Take it away," he sniffed. "And if you don't want an 'F' in this course, give me something I deem worthy of my time."

She walked quickly to her seat, a rush of heat in her head making her thoughts hard and sharp. Gathering her things with her hands shaking from anger, she turned and exited the class without looking at anyone. She held back her tears and bit at the insides of her cheeks until she tasted blood, just to keep her face steady and strong. What she had to say *did* matter, she knew it now, deep inside herself. Hedy would understand, and would be the best person to talk to about this. She knew her friend would see it in a clear way and have some ideas about what to do. She might even be proud of her for standing up for herself like she never did before. She hurried across campus and entered the bookstore quickly, hoping to get to her friend as soon as possible. They'd talk and get through the shelving work fast. It was still warm enough to barbecue, and she thought maybe Hedy would come over with Pauly for a few hamburgers. She could really use some wine and conversation.

But instead of Hedy behind the counter, it was Mrs. Boden, the store manager.

"Hedy in the back?" Eleanor asked, lifting a bottle of Coke out of the machine.

Mrs. Boden looked at her for a few second before saying anything. Then she started to cry.

"Oh Ellie, I just hate these kind of things," she said.

"Oh God," Eleanor said, already picking up her bookbag and slinging it back on her shoulder.

"Pauly called," Mrs. Boden said. "The officers were at the house. Something about a helicopter shot down over Tan Hung," she said. "Pleiku Province."

"Who was it?" Eleanor said over her shoulder.

"I don't know," Mrs. Boden answered, "Just tell her I'm so sorry."

But Eleanor had already dashed out the door, hurrying to get to her friend.

MIDGY AND TOMMY had gone next door. They knocked and nobody answered. But because they spent so much time together, Midgy opened the Percos' door and walked in. Pauly was sitting right there on the sofa, staring at nothing.

Tommy just stood there staring at Pauly. Midgy waited for him to look up, but he didn't. So, she talked first. "Pauly, is your mom here?"

Pauly turned to look at her in slow motion, "She's in the attic."

Midgy and Tommy climbed the steep stairs, ducking under the overhead beams, where they finally saw Hedy.

"Mrs. Perco?" Midgy said softly.

The two children moved toward her figure, there in the shadows. She was sitting on the planking, papers strewn across her lap, and spread across the floor.

Hedy watched Midgy and Tommy come toward her.

"I found it," she said, holding something out toward them.

When Midgy reached her, Hedy put something into her hands. It was an aged piece of red construction paper, frayed at the ends and weak along the folded lines. Around Hedy on the floor were workbook pages, report cards, school pictures. Vince Jr., 2nd grade, was written along the bottom of one of the photographs. Honor Roll certificates. Small clay figures made as art projects.

"He was such a smart boy," Hedy said quietly. "Always A's and B's. And a good baby. A very good baby."

Midgy looked at the paper in her hand. Tommy looked over her shoulder and read it for her.

"Happy Mother's Day from Vince, Jr.," he read.

There were two small handprints and a tiny poem. Beneath it, Tommy's finger followed what was written. "I hope that you will always be my mother," he read.

"I hold these little handprints," Hedy said, taking the paper back, "because he has to be somewhere, right? Even when the body's gone? He'll feel me holding on, wherever he is. I can't stand to think that he's alone."

Midgy didn't understand. She only stared at the way Hedy's shoulders seemed so small, and at the way her chest was shaking.

"I'm still his mother, damn it," Hedy said. "They can't kill that. They can't take that away."

Hedy stood slowly, she seemed to be moving through air too heavy for her body. She walked a few steps toward another old box, then looked at both the children for a few seconds without saying anything, like she was thinking of a language to speak in, as if she just realized they were there.

"Mrs. Perco," Midgy said. "Rachael said I have to tell you something."

"I took care of her," Tommy said.

Hedy listened to what the children had to say. Then she knelt down to Midgy, pulled her close and burst into tears.

"Please God, no," she said into Midgy's shoulder.

She lifted her face and looked at the child. "Don't be a woman, Midgy, please."

Midgy only stared at her. "Rachael said I didn't do anything wrong."

"It's got to stop somewhere, Midgy."

Midgy started to cry.

Tommy stepped toward them both, taking Midgy's hand in his own. "Why are you making her cry?" he said, "Why are you crying?"

"Because it will ruin everything. Women's bodies ruin everything."

Tommy looked frightened. "I don't want anything to happen to Midgy," he said.

"Then you watch out for her, Tommy. You help protect her from all of this," Hedy said. "Don't let her have any babies."

"I will," Tommy said, looking from Hedy to Midgy. "I promise I will."

"You're lying!" Midgy whispered, unsure. "Rachael said I didn't do anything wrong!"

"But you will," Hedy said. "We all do."

"I'll help," Tommy said.

"She's lying," Midgy said, beginning to cry again.

But Hedy failed to respond, and Midgy's words faded into the air around her. She watched as the older woman turned away from her and moved slowly without looking back toward the boxes beneath the eaves, opening them and concentrating on their contents, ignoring Midgy and Tommy as they stood watching. Finally, the children edged away from her, moving back down the stairs toward the living room. Pauly was still exactly as he was when they had left him; he didn't even look up when they entered the room again. The silence around the children was thickening. Shadows were gathering in the living room as the sun outside went down.

"Let's get out of here," Tommy said.

"Rachael said," Midgy whispered, moving closer to her friend.

"I promised," he nodded, still holding her hand, "and I will."

Through the door, Midgy saw the terrible silverblue flash of her mother's car as it pulled too quickly into the driveway. Something about the way her mother threw open the door, the way she rushed across the lawn, something about the stricken look on her face told Midgy big trouble was coming. Everything was very wrong and it was all her fault and now everyone would know. She held Tommy's hand and did not cry, waiting for the worst of what would happen, not even noticing how the light slanted scarlet across the land beyond the door, or how the sour gum tree out there on the lawn had turned the way she'd waited for, a blazing crimson red.

Memorial Day

NEAR BREAUX BRIDGE, LOUISIANA, three girls drove a faded red Cherokee off I-10 onto the packed dirt entrance of Frenchman's Creek Campground. This was the last Friday of May, 1973.

Valory, fresh from graduation at Cape Fear High, was at the wheel with a vengeance—sweat pooling between her breasts, driving into the scorching sun. Her older sister Rachael, nearly 23, sat beside her navigating as best she could. The battered Rand McNally Campground book on her sunburned legs kept flying up and flapping unevenly with the bumps and jostles of Valory's driving. In the back seat between piles of suitcases and food bags their cousin Marlena lay sleeping through the ride. Her auburn hair curled in wet waves around her face. She was 20 years old.

Barreling off the highway they plunged quickly into shadow. Moss hung thick on the trees and no sunlight filtered through to the forest floor. The campbook said Frenchman's Creek offered the best water sites and cleanest facilities, but not twenty yards off the main road the Cherokee was already running into low hung branches and skull-sized rocks. Carcasses of rotting forest animals lay along the sides of the road, their blood-dried fur writhing with maggots.

"It's gonna be hard to like this very much," Rachael said.

"Don't start," Valory answered. "We're stayin'."

She plowed on through tangles of undergrowth trying to read the faded road signs that led to the campground office.

This had been her idea: to leave North Carolina right after graduation to meet up with her runaway boyfriend, Tommy. He was playing mouth harp for Bobby "Big Man" Sadler's Blues Band in dirt road clubs through the Delta, calling himself T-Bone Hynes. Rachael and Marlena went along because they shared a suspicion that T-Bone wouldn't show and they didn't want Valory in some swamp spot all alone.

"Nobody said anything about leaving, Midget," Rachael said, using her dad's nickname for her sister. "I know the plan."

"Right," Marlena's voice came from the back seat. "Besides, we'all gotta die somewhere. And by the way, darlins': What fresh hell is *this*?"

They'd never laid eyes on Marlena 'til their grandmother's funeral in '63. Her father was their mother's brother with no love lost between them. They didn't see her again until '69 when she ran away from her father's home in Gretna, Alabama and found her way back to Fayetteville where they were living off-post at Fort Bragg. Off and on, she hung around go-go dancing in a topless bar that catered to enlisted men. Other times she went off to drive the highways searching town after town for the mother who left her when she was barely six years old.

"Welcome back, Dewdrop," Valory said to her. "Sleep well?"

"That all depends," Marlena said. "Are any of my formerly internal organs up there with you?"

"Not that I've seen," Valory said. She took one last two-wheeled curve and a battered, tumbledown building rose up from behind a clump of overgrown bushes.

"Then at some point I may require emergency assistance," Marlena yawned.

"La Revendeur Campstore" was handpainted in pine green strokes on a rotted board above a wood-framed screen door. A crippled old man sat on a bench outside, a near empty bottle of Echo Spring held loosely between his shaking knees.

Valory pulled the Jeep to a halt and they all climbed down to face him.

"You fine mam'selles here for the Cotillion?" he wheezed. Then his mouth opened in what looked to be a laugh, but without sound. His Adam's apple vibrated at the center of his skinny neck and spittle slid from the sides of his mouth. His shoulders shook.

The girls shot a glance between them and Valory stepped forward.

"We'd like a campsite," she said.

The old man looked them through, chewing his lip and squinting his right eye. He swallowed a gulp of bourbon.

"Ain't you seein' the sign off Rt. 10 down to the entrance?"

"No, sir," Rachael said.

"It says, 'Close for taxes,'" the old man said.

"Well what the hell does that mean?" Marlena said.

"Means we got shut down. Means IRS Federals sell everything, down to the toilet rolls in our stalls." He scratched the stubbly growth on his cheek while he talked.

"But you're still here," Valory said.

"Only four days, then new owners come."

"We've been driving eight hours," Valory said. "My camp book is old. It says this is a good place."

"It surely was, once on a time." The old man looked off into the growing darkness at the inky pine branches hanging low in the heat.

"Aw, hell," he said. "Other site still got folks. But you all promise: Clear out in three days. We all here illegal."

"Okay," Valory said, reaching into her wallet and handing him out some bills.

"No charge," he said, wiping the money away. "Bulldozers comin'."

Inside the store, deep in the shadow near the back wall of canned goods, the old man's middle-aged niece Veronique stood listening and watching through the rusted screen door. She had blue black hair and cheekbones like a Choctaw. Hers was a beautiful face, but attention was drawn to a puckered purple scar that ran from the left jawbone down the neck and right across the throat. Her long tanned fingers touched the scar now gently without thinking as she watched the three girls. They were all young and pretty but it was the one that climbed from the back, the one with auburn hair, her eyes clung to. Inside her chest was fluttering with what the Gris Gris women called The Motion of Knowing, and Veronique stood staring, a trance of some kind settling over her features.

Down road from the camp store buried deep in the thick trees of site 14, a canvas tent and battered old Airstream were circled by Harley Fat Boys and Custom Low-Riders. A rusted Chevy pickup with deer antlers attached to the front grill had a fully loaded gunrack on the back window, a busted up couch on the flatbed behind. From somewhere, an 8-track of Duane Allman's guitar licks sliced air that hung pungent with the taste of marijuana. Tattooed, bandana'd men sidled through the campsite, some so newly discharged they still wore military issue camouflage and dog tags. Some straddled their hogs and drank one-handed from long necked bottles. A few fed heroin habits they'd developed back in Nam, scattering syringes and spoons on the ground and nodding beneath the trees. They pissed openly onto the dusty ground leaving darkened lines and curves of urine-soaked earth. One of them called Cole Butler was a husky, dark-bearded Mississippi boy fresh from the battles of Nha Trang. He watched the red Cherokee pull by, raising Army field glasses to his face to spy on the three girls and the site they chose, studying each of them with a hungry interest as they piled out to the ground. He smiled, watching them pull their tent and supplies off the roof, with only the failing sun to light their work.

"We got neighbors," he announced to no one in particular. "And it's pussy."

He especially watched the one with the straight dark hair, liking the way it hung down to her waist like the schoolgirls in their white ao dais who traveled the streets of Saigon in the morning. Her hair stirred when she walked like Buddhist silk prayer flags in the wind. She stirred his memories of the young bar girls on those same Saigon streets under the neon lights of evening. VC Whores. He thought of the madame shaking her fist at him.

"You no come here no more!" she hollered. "You too much hurt my girls!"

He adjusted the focus on his field glasses to see the shape of the girl's breasts more clearly beneath the Indian print peasant shirt and felt a stiffening in his crotch as she reached to lift a box from the rack of the Cherokee, exposing a flash of tanned, tight belly.

He sucked air in through his teeth. "A mouthful o' me, momma," he said, "is surely what you need."

A smoke gray hound sidled up beside him panting slowly in the heat, a wheeze coming from his old chest. He dropped himself down in the dust pushing his head against Cole's leg.

From somewhere behind there came the sound of glass breaking, then cursing. Night was falling harder now and Cole saw the glow of cigarette tips shining orange in the darkness like tiny napalm flares.

RACHAEL HAD LIFTED her long brown hair and twisted it into a knot. Their tent was spread out on the ground before her, flat and unconquered.

"None of us know how to pitch this tent," she said. She crawled into the center and curled into a ball, tired from the scorching all-day sun and heat. "Let's just sleep on top of it, Midgy."

"These poles have everything to do with it," Valory said. "So, we'll figure it out." She was sorting them out by size and shape, trying to match them up with the diagrams on the paper insert that came in the tent box.

Marlena lounged at the picnic table where the kerosene lantern glowed with a quiet hiss. The old wooden table was covered with the resin of pine trees and peppered with fallen needles and cones. She was dressed in silk pajamas and matching sandals. Her hair was rolled and clipped over jumbo curlers the size of frozen lemonade cans. She sat blowing smoke rings into the air, repolishing her fingers and toes in the lamplight.

"Are you gonna help?" Valory asked her. "At all?"

"I'm plannin'," Marlena said. "on finding some men to put this tent up."

Valory looked quickly at her cousin. "Marly, I swear," she said, "You lure some redneck gorillas over here and I'll skin you alive. Rachael, talk to her."

"Who's talking redneck?" Marlena shrugged.

"Marly," Rachael said, motioning from her bed in the center of the tent fabric. "Does this look like a place to pick up boys from Princeton?"

"And just what would pale, pathetic rich boys from New Jersey know about anything a man needs to do?" Marlena said.

"No men, Marly," Valory repeated. "Pale, pathetic, or otherwise. Get off your pajamaed ass and pitch this tent with me."

"In silk? Besides, why isn't the fabulous Mr. T-Bone Hynes here, Valory? Why isn't his beautiful old self standing here ready to help us, eager with his muscles ripplin'?"

"He'll be here," Valory said. "Depend on it."

Marlena and Rachael shot a glance at each other and didn't answer.

"I saw that," Valory said. "Don't you two think I didn't."

They were pulled into a site that overlooked the Mississippi at a point wide enough to seem deep and a little dangerous. Heavy rains had muddied and swelled the current so that it moved fast, splashing thick over the slippery rocks that jutted up through the brown water.

From somewhere off in the growing darkness came a crack of thunder and the wail of a Jimi Hendrix riff. A cacophony of male sounds: talking, laughter, belches and shouts blended with the smell and sizzle of fresh meat cooking in flames. Once in a while the shatter of broken glass or the full-throttled roar of straight pipes, revved suddenly, exploded the birds from the trees, then went silent.

Valory stood up and stretched, watching the sky. "It's gonna storm again. Marly I mean it, you get over here silk or no silk. And Rach, you get yourself up off that tent and help me hold it up. Marly, slide the poles through the pockets. Rach, keep holding. I'll hammer the stakes into the ground and we'll all tie it down."

"And then, I'll definitely need to redo my nails," Marlena sighed, rising to obey.

OLD PORTER HAD ALREADY dragged his bench back inside the store and latched the rotted screen door behind him. Enormous gypsy moths fluttered madly around the yellow porch light. Their large wings scratched up against the store window and beat against each other. Then quickly consumed by the bulb's electric heat, their bodies melted into the summer air with barely a hiss to mark their passing from this world.

Veronique worked in the apartment behind the store readying a small supper of beans and pork. A shoebox of old photos lay on the table, a few set aside from the rest showed the same little wavy-haired girl from toddler to about five years old posed in front of Christmas trees or backyard bushes, sitting dangle-legged on a couch or smiling into the camera from a tricycle on a sidewalk.

Old Porter limped into the back nodding to his niece. Five years ago in '68, she'd shown up at his door straight from a long hospital stay in Tennessee. Her throat had been cut during riots in Memphis, the summer King was killed. She'd been beaten and raped and busted up pretty bad and asked her uncle for a place to hide herself away for a while. She was the daughter of Porter's youngest sister who'd turned whore in Alabama, somewhere up near Dennersfield. And when his niece showed up at the campground, she was still bruised and disfigured and nobody knew if she'd stay that way for good. Porter felt real bad and took her in, let her help with what she could. But now hard times were sending them both back out to the world. At least, Old Porter thought while he watched her set the table, her face had healed up real beautiful again. That was something.

She waited for him to move slowly into the room before talking. "Those girls you let stay?" she began.

He nodded. "I knowed I shouldn't."

"They sign the camp book?"

Porter squinted his eyes at her and drew back his head. "What the hell for?"

Veronique kept her face down, arranging the plates. "One of them's my daughter."

Porter sat slowly at the table staring at her. "How you tell that?" he asked. "Ain't it near on fifteen years?"

"You mark me," she said, pushing the photographs toward him. "Her name's Marlena Galloway."

IT POURED THROUGH THE NIGHT. Inside their tent the girls moved their sleeping bags far away from the zipper flap where little blasts of wet wind still made it through. The bags of groceries lined up against one wall of the tent were getting soggy from the damp air. Lightning flashed and thunder cracked too soon afterwards, telling them that the strikes were coming down close. The roar of the Mississippi nearly at their feet threatened to flood its banks and pull them all downstream. Through this they lay awake together, staring up through the darkness, barely talking. It was nearly three a.m. when a beam of a flashlight struck the wall of the tent and they watched as it looped and lifted around in the air, as if being carried by someone having a hard time walking through the weather.

"Finally!" Valory whispered, sitting up and crawling toward the zippered flap, "T-Bone's here."

The light was right at the front now and she unzipped quickly, the other girls making room to let him inside fast without the storm following.

But it was Cole Butler in a camouflage poncho, squatting at the entrance and shining his light into the girls' stunned faces.

"Don't mean to frighten you, ladies. Just thought you could use somebody givin' a looksee, checkin' if you all were okay."

"We're just fine," Marlena snapped.

"My boyfriend is on his way," Valory added.

Rachael covered her bare legs with the sleeping bag and hugged her pillow to her chest.

Cole glanced over at her and smiled. "I won't disturb you, then," he said. "Just thought it could be a little frightening here, with you all alone."

"My boyfriend's coming," Valory said again.

Cole kept his eyes on Rachael. "Yeah," he said. "Well, goodnight."

He stood and backed away.

Valory zipped the opening closed again quickly. "Shit," she said, looking at the other two. "Shit and god-damned shit."

Outside, Cole stood awhile in the downpour, his flashlight off and stashed in a flap of his poncho. He moved carefully to a spot beneath a large oak and hesitated, glancing again at the tent. Then he reached up, grabbed a branch and swung himself silently into the tree. Like a jungle animal, he climbed swiftly through the wet branches to a place high above the girls' tent where he was able to watch whatever went on for as long as he felt the need.

THE BIRDS STARTED an infernal racket about 5 a.m. and it was barely dawn when Valory unzipped the opening of the tent quietly and stepped outside. The rains had stopped and morning began with a silver edge of newly-washed light. She opened the back of the Jeep and removed a green metal camp stove, set it on the picnic table and went to fill a coffee pot with water from the hook-up. The river still rushed and splashed noisily. It would take several days without rain for it to slow down now.

Marlena was next to emerge, her curlers askew and her silk pajamas wrinkled like accordion pleats. She glanced over at Valory, standing at the water spout, and sat slowly at the picnic table holding her head in her hands.

"Why my God," she said. "did I ever agree to this?"

"Nobody forced you," Valory said, counting the scoops of coffee into the pot and setting it on the camp stove.

"Well, he's still not here, is he?"

Valory shrugged. "He will be."

There was silence between them as the coffee began to perk. The birds had quieted down some, and a heavy warmth had already begun to thicken the air.

"That asshole scared the shit out of me last night," Marlena said.

"I'm so sick of soldiers," Valory agreed, "I could spit."

"Try wiggling your bare tits in front of them for a living," her cousin yawned.

"The hell with your tits," Valory said. "Try being the daughter of Roy Meade."

"Oh yeah," Marlena said. "I guess you win."

Valory and Rachael's father had been in Southeast Asia since '56, long before the U.S. government admitted to having anything more than advisors in Saigon. But Roy Meade was no advisor. Roy Meade was a warrior. Valory called him "a paint your face, lurk in the mud, throat-cutting, weapon wielding, highly-trained Special Forces/MACVSOG covert operative," and not entirely without pride in her voice. The military listed him as MIA in '69, but his wife and daughters suspected that it was just an official ruse to let him go further underground, freeing him to act outside the confines of official military sanction.

The cousins drank their coffee hungrily.

"How long since we've eaten?" Valory wondered.

"Who cares? I'm doing black beauties," Marlena said. "But don't tell Rachael."

Valory leaned away from her cousin. "Damn it, Marly. You promised no more dexies."

Marlena shrugged. "I was getting fat."

"Bullshit," Valory said. "My right leg weighs more than your whole body."

"Can we change the subject?" Marlena said. "Wouldn't you kill for a shower?"

COLE HAD BEEN DOZING when the sound of stirring on the ground below woke him. As silent as a rock, he watched and listened.

"Asshole," he heard them say.

"VC bitches," he muttered.

Then he waited, watching them gather their things for the showers. He heard them decide to let Rachael sleep. He liked knowing her name. A little longer he waited, watching with his field glasses until he saw them disappear into the red cedar bath building.

Finally, with trained stealth, he slid from the tree and moved silently across the site to the tent. A swift and quiet entry and he stood before Rachael where she lay sleeping. In the growing heat she had kicked her legs free of the sleeping bag and slept in a t-shirt and panties. Cole stared at her long tanned legs and tight ass, the breasts that lifted with her breath. He knelt now, straddling her, his hands already holding her shoulders and his weight about to crush itself into her. That was when she woke, her eyes opening to stare directly into his bearded face. He grabbed her quickly by the throat before she could make a sound and yanked her panties down with the other hand. She thrashed beneath him as much as she could but he was already pushing his way into her body. Her legs were pinned beneath his bulk—she couldn't kick at him, she couldn't move at all except to twist her chest and shoulders, going nowhere, then trying to bite his arm, her teeth sinking into his flesh, tearing at it ferociously, his hand still nearly crushing her throat, his thrusts already growing faster, tearing her insides.

Suddenly a blast and he was down, fallen heavily onto her, flopping like a whale. Another blast and by now Rachael had moved her head from beneath his and knew it was Valory moving toward them, putting the gun to the back of his skull and blasting again. His eyes looked into Rachael's with one last look of astonishment. His head shattered, blood and flesh and bone flying everywhere, blood on their bodies, blood all over the tent. Blood pooling from his head and flowing, seeping into the sleeping bag, making a river that poured itself wherever it could go. Rachael tried to breathe but couldn't, and then she could and she was screaming. This time it was Valory's hand on her mouth, pushing at her bloody face.

"Shhhh, DON'T," she said.

"Help me, oh my God," Rachael gagged, trying to free herself from the corpse, and it wouldn't move.

"Wait," Valory said, grabbing a beefy shoulder and shoving, pushing from one side so that the mass slid across the slick film of its own blood and landed in a heap against the tent wall. The penis was still dark and partially engorged. Rachael scrambled away, beginning to vomit.

"Oh my god," she said, her body heaving, vomit mixing with the blood on the tent floor. "He's killed."

"So?" Valory said.

"He's dead, Valory. He's really dead."

"He was rapin' you, Rachael," Valory said, kneeling down to her sister's side.

"It would have been over soon," Rachael said. "It would have been okay."

"Are you insane?" Valory said. "I shot the bastard. He's dead. I'd like to shoot him some more."

Rachael vomited again as Valory held her shoulders. Then she let her sister guide her out of the tent to the bank of the rushing river. Valory cupped the muddy water in her hands and tried to wash the blood from Rachael's legs and face and hair.

"The gun," Rachael said. "Where . . . ?"

"Dad's," Valory said. "The one from mom's night table."

It was a Smith and Wesson .38 caliber handgun. She'd come back for her knapsack, she said, and saw Cole on her sister. She'd grabbed the gun and shot, aiming as best she could. Now as she washed the thick stickiness off her sister's body, she searched for signs that a bullet might have grazed Rachael herself.

"Is this all his blood?" she asked.

"I think so. I can't tell. I don't know what to do, Midgy, what are we going to do?"

"Clear out," Valory said. "We'll go get Marlena and haul ass out of here."

"And leave him in there?"

"You got any better ideas?"

"I don't know what to do. I can't think at all."

"Then let me handle this, and do what I say," Valory said.

She led Rachael by the shoulders, helping to steady her as they headed up to the camp store and baths. She had been careful to zip the tent, doing her best to keep the contents from attracting the attention of animals who might smell the blood.

VERONIQUE HEARD THE GUN BLASTS as she was hanging laundry behind the store.

"Idiots," she muttered. "God-damned brain addled dickheads."

They'd been camped there for weeks, shooting through the forest every day, littering their site with liquor bottles and syringes, littering the campground with small dead animals and birds. She hadn't wanted them there. But Porter felt sorry, knowing they'd been discharged from a military hell, come home to where they were hated and reviled.

"They got no future in America," he said to his niece. "They don't belong nowhere. What's the harm in a few days?"

"There's no way to answer that question," she said. "These guys could be capable of anything."

"Let 'em run wild for a while," Porter said. "I heard tell when a dog's been beat real bad, that's what you do: let 'im run. Brings him back to hisself. Then he can be retrained."

"Well, I trust dogs a lot more than I trust men," his niece answered.

And Porter didn't try arguing her down on that.

She turned from hanging the second basket of wet clothes in time to see the two girls come around the side of the bath house. One was stumbling, nearly naked, and blood-soaked. The other was guiding her, bloody herself, but clearly in more command of the situation. Marlena was not with them. Without thinking, Veronique ran toward them, her heart pounding in her throat.

"Hey!" she yelled. "Where's the other girl?"

The sisters stood still, watching her bolt in their direction. This was the first they'd seen of this woman, and she ran like a cheetah across the open lot, reaching their side in seconds.

"The third," she said, breathless. "Where is she?"

"In the showers," Valory said, frowning. "Who are you?"

Veronique looked into their faces and knew who they were. These were Eleanor's girls, her daughter's cousins.

"We killed someone," Rachael said to her.

"I killed him," Valory corrected. "She was being raped at the time."

Veronique listened to their story. Then she laid out a plan: get Marlena, stay together, clean themselves up. Bundle their bloody clothes and meet her back at the camp store. Don't separate. She got them to the door of the bath house, then she walked down the dirt road, heading to site #14.

One of the soldiers was sprawled on a picnic table, whether asleep or drugged she couldn't tell. Two others sat on the couch in the flatbed cleaning their rifles and drinking beer. A few dogs roamed the site, digging at the ground or stretching out their bodies in the shade.

"Where's the rest of you?" she asked, coming up on them from the side.

"Hey, it's the Lady of the Forest," the blond one said. "What can we do for you, Pretty Lady? You want more money?"

"We never took money from any of you," she said. "I'm here because there were Feds here last night, looking around."

"Shit," said the one whose head was shaved.

"They were flashing some pictures," she said, "saying how there was heroin out here."

"Fuck," said the blond.

"That bearded one . . . what's his name?"

"You mean Cole? What about him?"

"Came by the store first thing this morning," she said, looking right in their faces. "I mentioned this to him, and he took off. Stole my outboard and headed upriver."

"That son of a bitch."

"I think you all need to clear out right away. I don't want trouble here." She turned to leave, and glanced back at them. "Find the others and get yourselves gone fast. That's what I came to say."

OLD PORTER LAY IN BED. Used to be that dawn never found him under the sheets. But these days there didn't seem to be much reason to move in any direction. His window was opened wide and the early light was shining onto the bedspread that lay pushed to the bottom of his bed. He looked at his gnarled old legs; they'd lost most their muscle and were nothing more than sagging skin and ancient bone. He leaned his elbows into the mattress and hauled himself up to sitting, leaning his head against the wood of the backboard and watching Veronique carry the first basket of laundry to the line. She was clipping a sheet tight and straight when he heard the first shot ring the air. He closed his eyes, knowing that his niece had been right about those boys. They were more hopeless than ruined animals. Hate was too deep inside them now. He felt the second shot vibrate in his heart and throat and heard the horrible blast of the third. It tired him out and he rolled back onto his side, fearing the kind of world he was going to be living in outside the campground borders. He thought of his little sister, Veronique's mother, dead now, long dead. His other brothers and sisters, gone too. What good is family, he wondered, if it ends up being nothing more than a hole inside of you nothing can fill? What good is any of it, he wondered. When it's all over and ended, what good has any of it been?

In the bath house Marlena listened, ferociously plucking her eyebrows as her cousins detailed what had happened. While they showered she walked to the campsite, promising to bring them a change of clothes from the suitcases in the car. Moving toward the tent she could already smell the flesh inside as it began to stink in the heat. She stood briefly staring at the tent door, then turned away.

Fiercely and quickly she moved around the campsite, repacking everything outside the tent back into the Cherokee. She climbed into the driver's seat and drove the car a few hundred yards away, leaving the engine idling. Then she ran back to the tent, a gallon tin of kerosene swinging in her clenched fist. Without hesitation she emptied the contents around the edge of the tent. She splashed it across the fabric of the roof, down the sides, into the screen flaps to wet what lay inside. When she tossed the match flames roared to life, already spreading. In the time it took her to run back to the waiting car and throw it into gear, the fire was already tearing upward through the air.

"Are you NUTS?" Valory screamed at her.

"What is the matter with you?" Rachael asked, unbelieving.

"Just get dressed and shut up," Marlena said, throwing their clothes at them. "We've got to get the hell out of here now."

"We can't get out of here, Marly," Rachael said. "What about the old man and the woman?"

"What woman?" Marlena asked.

Valory had already run through the entrance, heading for the camp store.

VERONIQUE HAD RETURNED from site 14 and was telling her uncle the details of the killing.

"I cleared the others out," she said. "This way, we can clean it up. No interference."

Old Porter was standing at the screen door still in his pajamas, his back to her as she talked. He was watching the black curls of smoke fill the air a few hundred yards down road. Tentacles of flame were beginning to rise higher.

"I don't see cleanin' it up to be an easy thing from where I stand," he said.

His niece walked to the door and stood staring over Porter's shoulder.

"Marlena," she said, crossing her arms tightly over her chest.

They let it burn. It wasn't possible to do anything else. A fire department come too soon would have put out the fire and found the body. It was clear once Veronique explained it to them all that the burning, once it had been started, had to be allowed to run its course. To be sure that the remains would be nothing but a pile of unrecognizable rubble, she said, they'd have to wait it out.

"She always does this," Valory said, motioning to her cousin. "She burned her own house down when she was five."

"I'm sure that was an accident," Veronique said quietly.

"Thank you," Marlena said. "It was." She had been staring into this woman's face ever since they had entered the camp store. She studied the puckered scar that ran down her throat; she watched her lips; she noted the curve of the eyebrows and the way that one arched higher than the other.

"We're not going to just sit here and let this whole campground burn down, are we?" Rachael asked.

"It'll stop at the river, if the wind's right," Porter said.

He looked around him at the place where he'd spent most of his life. The sawdust floor, the slant of morning light, shelves stocked with camp supplies, first aid kits, canned goods. He looked at his niece, so unflinching and capable in a moment like this. And these girls, two of them solid as young mountains, the third a tangled wilderness. Each of them, he felt certain, already dedicated to their own brand of trouble. Family, he thought, the word springing through his mind and crouching there, squat in the middle of all other ideas, liable to jump in any direction.

At one point during their waiting, the old black deskphone near the register began to ring. Porter picked it up suspiciously, and listened.

He looked at the girls. "Anybody here want to talk to a guy called T-Bone?"

Valory put her hands on the edge of the counter and pushed herself out on a slant. Then she stopped and looked long through the screen door at the burning landscape. She cut her glance back to Porter and shook her head.

"Just tell him we're gone," she said. "And don't explain anything."

FIREMEN FROM THE BREAUX BRIDGE station picked through the charred grounds half-heartedly. It was a holiday weekend after all and they wanted to be home with their families, having their own good times.

"Just discharged," Veronique told them, shrugging. "Half-crazed, most of them."

"Long gone, too, I expect," Porter added, shaking his head.

The three girls had been bundled back into the Cherokee and sent north before the fire trucks came.

"Just keep going 'til you get there," Veronique said. "And don't ever look back to this time with anybody but each other."

She made them promise. "Secrets are what hold people together," she said, "whether we like it or not."

Through the hours of the ride home, a weighted quiet settled on them all.

"Nothing will ever feel the same again," Rachael said.

"It will," Valory said. "Once this is the sameness we mean."

Marlena had nothing to say. It wasn't until the jeep had crossed the state line into Georgia that she reached again to feel the contents of her pocket. While Veronique settled them into the car, Porter had slipped something into her hand.

"It ain't my place to do more," he whispered.

She'd wait 'til she was alone to look again. For now she'd feel it, imagine it with the tips of her fingers: the fading colors, the younger Veronique—in her arms the little girl Marlena knew to be herself. In her mother's young face, in that innocence, Marlena tried to imagine a different fate for them all.

Ronnie, Marlena's father called her.

"Ronnie," her father must have said.

And she smiled in his direction, their child in her arms. But what could it mean? In the face of the younger Veronique, Marlena saw no thought of leaving, just as in today's Veronique, she saw no thought of return.

Marlena's fingers lingered on the surface of the photograph. The jeep traveled on, Valory driving them now toward home. It would stay within her forever: the memory of this Veronique who stood silently and watched Marlena go. But what of this younger Veronique, hugging her baby close and smiling in hope—hope, which is stronger than love—smiling toward the camera as if it were the future, as if there was nothing more to see?

"Maybe it will all be okay," Rachael said, interrupting her cousin's thoughts. "Do you think that could be true?"

No one made reply. They were too tired, each in their own way. All too changed to believe anything would be easy, ever again. Still, they knew enough to let this prayer of hope circle close above them like a hawk that hunts at dawn, with its hunger and determination, surely, to follow them all the way home.

What We Love

WE WERE NEAR TO AIKEN, low on fuel and lost on our way to Columbia. Bina declared she would not drive another mile without sleep, so we checked into a roadside spot called something like the Our Place Motel. The parking lot was empty except for one broken-down flatbed truck loaded with dead tree stumps and a bumper sticker that claimed, "Rednecks Rule!" The girl behind the desk in the office was about 17 years old, bleary eyed at nearly 1a.m., and fat as a mama hog. She wore a Big Brother and the Holding Company T-shirt over what I finally realized was about the most pregnant stomach I'd ever seen.

"Y'all have to jiggle that key a whole lot or it'll never work," she yawned. "And just yell if you got brown water. I'll be there in a flash."

The key stuck in the lock a few times before we could get the door open and once we did, the smell of mildew just about knocked us over.

"Christ, it's a mess," Bina said.

There were two double beds, both with collapsed and uneven mattresses, and except for one wall-lamp between the headboards, none of the lights in the room worked.

"Well, we're here now," Charlie said, setting her bags down and stretching her arms above her head. "May as well make the best of it."

"As long as we spray ourselves down with Lysol in the morning," Bina called.

She was already in the bathroom washing her big-toed feet in the sink—she had a thing about clean feet at bedtime.

"Water's sort of beige," she yelled. "So I guess it's not too bad."

"Static must be popular around here," I answered. "'Cause that's all I'm getting on this radio."

Charlie was smoothing out the wrinkles of her clothes for the next day. She said, "Valory, you're the film major. What's that Hitchcock movie this place seems like?

Above the whistle of the water pipes, Bina hollered. "Who the hell has to be a film major to know that?"

We were on our way to see Charlie's fiancé Owen who was stationed in Fort Jackson. We'd cut some classes at Georgia State to make it a long weekend. Charlie talked about this fiancé since we started school together in the fall. He'd been a gas station attendant at his father's BP station near Valdosta, GA last year in '73 and Charlie spent her senior year in high school driving around.

I frowned, "Wasting gas in the middle of the gas shortage? Just so you could buy some more and see him for a while?"

"It was worth it," she said. "We got engaged, didn't we?"

"Was that some kind of promotional deal?" Bina asked.

"Yea," I said. "Buy fifty tanks of gas, get an engagement ring?"

We were in my dorm room when she told us about that, heating up some tomato soup on an illegal hotplate.

"No, silly. We just figured we'd do it before he left for basic training."

"Basic training for what?" I asked. "Doesn't he know the war's been cancelled?" That was Autumn '73. Vietnam was over as far as most Americans were concerned.

"That's what makes it perfect," Charlie said. "He'll get all the benefits and none of the inconvenience."

"Inconvenience?" I repeated.

My father had been in Special Forces since 1955.

"Did she say '*inconvenience*'?" I said, beginning to raise my voice.

"Don't freak," Bina said. "People don't know."

I stopped myself before I could get all the way to mad. Bina was right. I grew up in a world that could have been another planet as far as most of the country was concerned: Fort Bragg, North Carolina. Fayettenam, some people called it. And in that world everybody knew the suffering of the war. Everybody had a father, a son, a brother, there. New soldiers were flown out just as often as the caskets of dead soldiers were flown in. Bina knew about it now that she lived with me because roommates know so much so fast. In those first few days of loneliness, you smoke a lot of grass and say a lot of stuff. Of course, there are secrets I'll never tell. But there's plenty to share anyway. For instance, I knew Bina was really named Jobina Lipson, the adopted daughter of Methodist parents from Wichita. Mrs. Lipson quoted scripture and ironed to relax. Mr. Lipson built model ships and cried too easily. Our first night in the dorm room together she told me.

"Picture a grown man," Bina said, handing me a joint, "sobbing through a Gene Autry record. His wife's quoting Isaiah and ironing ferociously in the corner."

"Where are you in that picture?" I asked, holding a hit and passing the joint back.

"Exactly," she inhaled.

Charlie lived across the hall alone. She was a German language major and her parents actually paid extra for a single room thinking that would make her study more. Through family connections, she had a job waiting for her at the West German Embassy in D.C. and they didn't want her to blow it. But she was lonely and always hung with us.

That's why we were the ones who drove her to South Carolina. Bina had a car, a tiny yellow Austin American. It got the best gas mileage so we wouldn't have to spend too much money; but it looked like a toaster on roller skate wheels and couldn't go over 45 without vibrating like an epileptic. So the trip took longer than expected and we were all pretty tired. Good thing, too, or the mildew smell and terrible state of the room we were in would have kept us all awake. Besides that, the guy with the flatbed truck was blasting Iron Butterfly in the room next door and we could hear it right through the walls as we were settling down to bed.

"How the hell did *he* get a station?" I wondered.

"If we can be up by 6, we'll be riding through the gates of Fort Jackson in time to take Owen to lunch," Charlie said.

The Our Place sign glowed red in our window as we turned off the wall-lamp. The glow splashed across the mounds our legs made under the threadbare blankets.

"Nothin' doin'," Bina said. "Owen takes us to lunch. I'm not paying for some military dick to stuff his ugly face."

"Enlisted men don't make much money," Charlie said. "And he's not ugly. I told you a million times, he looks a little like George Maharis."

"I have no idea who that is," Bina said.

"For heaven's sake," Charlie said. "He played Buzz Murdock on Route 66. Didn't you ever watch TV as a kid?"

"We didn't have one in the house," Bina said. "My mother said it was the Devil's box."

"Well that explains a few things," I said.

"Anyway," Charlie said. "Owen looks like George Maharis, only with a little more weight to his face and a broken nose from a wrestling injury."

"Stop talkin' or you'll give me nightmares," Bina said, punching her pillow. "This thing smells like the inside of my old gym locker."

I banged on the wall and the guy next door turned down "Inagadadavida" just in time to spare us the drum solo.

"I must be crazy, coming down here," Bina said.

"Is that your professional opinion?" I asked.

Bina was a psychology major, wanting to be a head doctor. I always thought she'd make a better Mother Superior. She spent most of her energy trying to convince the two of us girls to stay away from the campus collection of guys. She felt they were inferior and would only get in the way of our higher goals. I wasn't much different than Charlie, though. My higher goal was to get Tommy Buonorotti to marry me. I'd been in love with him since we were kids together at Bragg. I had three more years at school, if I stayed, and he was a high school drop out, blowing mouth harp in blues bars between Memphis and New Orleans, calling himself T-Bone Hynes.

He called me every Monday and Thursday night from pay phones at the clubs. I had given him an old Mixture 79 Tobacco can filled with my dad's Indian Head nickel collection so he'd have the change.

I kept hoping he'd want me to come and stay with him. Finally, the night before our trip with Charlie I came right out and asked him. Something inside me was just ripping me up.

He said, "You should finish college, Midget."

"That's three more years!" I said. "Are you crazy?"

"I've got no place," he said. "I'm on the road."

"So I'll come on the road."

"And be what?"

That stopped me cold. I didn't know what he meant.

"This is what I want," he said. "The music. It's what I can be. What I am."

"And?"

"What are YOU?" he asked.

I didn't know what to say.

"You gotta care about something," he said.

"I care about you," I said. "Jeez."

"Not that," he said. "Your mom never cared about a damn thing but Roy and look what it got her."

"I'm not her, damn you. And don't talk about Roy."

"You gotta love something besides me, Midget," he repeated.

"You're just scared, Tommy Bones," I told him.

"Probably," he said. "But I'm right, too."

So what the hell should I love? I wanted to find something fast so Tommy'd change his mind and take me with him—something manageable that wouldn't get in the way of the goal that Tommy didn't like me having. I belonged with him is how I saw it.

So that's what I was lying in that damp bed thinking about once things settled down. Then before I could fall asleep all the way, Charlie got up again in the dark. She tiptoed into the bathroom without turning on the light and was in there for a while doing I didn't know what. Turns out she was blind-shaving her legs in anticipation of being with her boyfriend the next day. The water was a thin trickle, little more than a dripping out of the faucet. She had no shaving cream, so she was dragging the razor up her legs with the determination only a girl in a state of obsession can have. She probably thought we were sleeping but even in the next room we could hear the scraping so loud we couldn't stand it.

Bina yelled, "Charlie, for Christ sake, what the hell are you doing?"

"Damn," Charlie said, snapping on the light switch, "I didn't want to wake you guys. I nearly forgot to shave my legs."

"Well, you're gonna hit bone," I said. "and it's kinda hard to sleep through a ritual self-slaughter."

Charlie stuck her leg out the bathroom door. "Hardly any blood at all," she said, wiggling her toes and flexing the leg muscles she had from playing Girls' Team Tennis.

"How many times do I have to tell you two: shaving our legs is succumbing to the patriarchal ideal," Bina growled. "Free yourselves."

Bina herself was hairy as a Yeti. And for my part, I thought it looked like hell. But Bina acted as if everything she did was right and that she had the authority to push it down your throat if you wouldn't swallow. For instance, Charlie's real name was Charlotte, which Bina decided right away was not acceptable.

"Sugary names like Charlotte just get girls into trouble," she declared. "Charlie is your name from now on."

"Okay, Bina," Charlie said. "I'll try to remember."

So anyway that was the three of us on that February weekend in '74. We were up the next morning, Charlie saw to it, and on the road at the crack of dawn. We gassed up and bought a quart of orange juice to share. I got one of those boxes of twelve doughnuts, the ones that had four plain, four white sugar, four cinnamon. It was an empty box of crumbs by the time we pulled into Columbia. It was so warm that day we couldn't believe it was only February. The air smelled like moist earth and felt warm on our faces. We checked into the Heart of Columbia Motel, which after the dump in Aiken felt like a high price resort, or at least what a trio of know-nothing state college girls might imagine a high price resort to be. There were maids rolling their cleaning carts from room to room, calling to each other and laughing. Used sheets were bundled in piles and the hum of vacuums mingled with the songs of birds—sounded to me like some chickadees and maybe a blue warbler—perched in the branches of the Loblolly Pines. We threw our suitcases into the room and headed right away to Fort Jackson.

Driving through the gates of the post gave me a familiar and slightly sick feeling in my stomach that I'd been trying hard to get away from. It felt too much like Bragg here: that buried alive feeling, with rows of squat, dark military boxes for the soldiers. Camouflage trucks. Camouflage jeeps. Camouflage men. Lots of men. Lots of death certificates.

There were soldiers everywhere, all staring at us in that starvin' way that makes you feel stripped naked and licked all over by somebody with puked-up beer breath. Charlie giggled about it because she was nervous and Bina started getting hostile, flashing her rump at guys as they passed. I did nothing, not reacting in any way, keeping my eyes focused off in the distance as if I wasn't really here, which is basically how I preferred to feel around anything to do with the military world.

Driving through the post, we searched for the area where the barracks might be. Finally, we found them. There were long lines of Quonset huts with identifying letters and numbers. We searched out the boyfriend's barracks and sent some blond-haired private in to bring him out. We got out of the car and waited, watching the other enlisted men in their military issue, their pants tucked into their big black boots, walking heavily across the grounds.

I pointed to a few of the men. "If the pants are bloused out around the boots that way, it means they've passed airborne training," I said.

"It's so damned weird that you know stuff like that," Bina said. "God."

"Bina, the tonnage of what I know," I said, and stopped myself.

"Like what?" she said.

"Forget it," I said. Secrets. So many secrets.

Then Owen walked out the door of his barracks. He stood for a while frowning at the three of us, then came to the street with a stone face that looked as if he were about to order our executions.

"Charlotte, what the hell are you doin' here?" he asked.

Confused, we waited, leaning on Bina's little yellow car.

"Didn't you get my letter?" he frowned.

"Of course I got that silly letter," Charlie said, "Why do you think I'm here?"

"This won't accomplish anything," he said. "I meant what I said. The engagement's off."

Bina and I looked at Charlie, then at each other.

"I liked it better when I didn't know what was going on," Bina said.

"I don't know what to do," I whispered.

One glance at Charlie and it was clear she was going to cry. And this boyfriend just stood stiffly, first on one leg then the other, looking around like maybe he wanted another dimension to open up and swallow us down.

"Charlotte . . . ," he said.

"Her name is Charlie," Bina fired back.

"He can call me what he likes," Charlie said.

What I saw in Charlie's face then was iron determination. She was a plump girl with a kind of round prettiness that would have fit well into Austrian peasant dresses. She looked like the bargirl on those German beer labels: blonde, rosy-cheeked, buxom and eternally pleasant. This determination was something new, and I realized that she believed her whole life hung on the next few hours of time.

Bina, with her mental block against romantic love, missed it.

I moved a little ways away from the couple and motioned to Bina. "You need to come here," I said.

She looked at me for a minute about to resist, but thought better of it for some reason and walked over to me.

"I want to get her out of here," she said.

"You leave her alone," I said. "I mean it."

"This is disgusting. I'm embarrassed for her."

"You don't give her enough credit. She's no pushover."

Bina didn't like the fact that I was contradicting her. But in the time it took for us to have our talk, Charlie had convinced this guy that we should all make a day of it which proved me right about her. The boyfriend told us he had a friend who was not stationed at Jackson, a civilian who lived in Sumter, just a ways off, in a house that withstood slavery and The War.

"He works in a hardware store in town, and gets off in a little while," he told us.

"The War?" Bina frowned.

I looked at Owen. "She's not from the South."

The friend, whose name was Kevin Joe, came a while later and turned out to be very shy around women. It wasn't because he was bad looking or anything. He was pretty cute actually with light brown hair and a pair of chocolate button eyes that glistened in the sunlight. He was lean, but not scarecrow skinny like some Southern boys can be, with just enough meat to make it matter, is how I'd put it. But he was so quiet. He wouldn't look us in the face as he opened the car door for us all. He drove a multi-colored '66 Bonneville Convertible which his friends called "Frankenstein," because it was patched together from the bodies of a few different cars.

"It was in a dead-wreck so I got it real cheap," he said quietly. "I'm saving up to have it painted one color."

"A lofty goal," Bina whispered to me.

The drive was a quiet one, with Charlie trying to keep some talk going for a while. But it died too many times, so she began looking out the window and dabbing her nose with a used tissue. A country station was playing on the radio and we heard some old Patsy Cline, Loretta Lynn and a Merle Haggard. Bina was rolling her eyes at me every ten seconds. I couldn't tell if it was because of all the emotion in the front seat, or the country music.

"Psychologists have compassion," I told her.

"Only the inexpensive ones," she shrugged.

We were off the highway by then, pulling down a long dirt road that turned out to be a drive which led to Kevin Joe's house. We rounded a bend and I saw the remains of a real plantation house, the likes I had never seen up close before. It stood at the end of two lines of giant sycamores. Its portico was now just a row of unpainted Greek pillars and a partially collapsed roof. The dirt yard was filled with skinny dogs, slinking on their bellies as the car kicked up the pebbles and dust. I looked at Kevin Joe's face and saw that he was in love; he looked at this place with the awe reserved for our feelings of the divine. He stopped the car and got out slowly, raising himself from the driver's seat without ever taking his eyes off the structure. I began to see it, too—a kind of magic that hung in the air, even in the collapse of glory, or maybe because of it—because in the collapse of everything that passes for glory there remains that which is truly glorious.

All I've ever known was on-post housing and then rented off-post housing. Nothing ever felt like it belonged to us. We never felt like we belonged anywhere. This was different, I could feel it right away. It was something that couldn't disappear or die.

Only Charlie and Owen were still in the car.

Bina was leaning against the trunk of the Bonneville—this part of the car was a light metallic green—facing away toward the road. She was saying out loud to no one in particular, "Do we have to be anywhere like this, really?" over and over without expecting an answer.

Kevin Joe looked over and caught me watching the same thing he was in love with.

"Do you want to see more?" he said. "I mean you don't have to or anything."

"Sure," I said, and meant it.

We walked the grounds toward the front porch. Kevin Joe pointed out the trees.

"We got some real old beauties here," he said to me. "Over there's a Sparkleberry Tree. And around back we got some Shagbark Hickories."

"I've been learning about birds from a course at Georgia State," I said. "But don't know much about trees, except for a sour gum tree I remember as a kid."

"Trees are real easy," he said, warming up to me now. "The leaves and the bark are what you need to know."

He pointed out a Kentucky Coffeetree and some Tamarisk. "We even got a Quakin' Aspen," he said. "I think that's my favorite."

We had come up to the entrance of the house by now.

"The steps are a little dangerous" Kevin Joe said.

He guided us—because now everyone decided they might as well follow—to the safe places for our feet.

"Otherwise," he said, "the old wood just won't bear up."

He opened the big double front doors and led us into an entrance hall that was bigger than our whole freshman lounge. There was a spiral stairway and marble tile floors, once magnificent but now filthy with dust and mud. A chandelier the size of a Jupiter moon hung above us dangling webs filled with spiders and other dead bugs. On either side of this hall there were thick pocket doors, the kind that open into the walls and disappear. Kevin led us first through one set, into the "ballroom," a stadium-sized empty room.

"There used to be parties," he said, "long ago. Cotillions were sometimes held here, weddings."

Charlie finally began to cry.

"Jesus Christ," Bina said.

"Oh," Kevin Joe said, looking at the boyfriend. "Sorry."

Owen shrugged, "It's okay."

"Says who?" Bina snarled.

"I didn't expect her to react like this," he said.

"Well she did, and she's here and maybe you should take her someplace to talk instead of dragging us over here to some death-infested ruin just to pass the time hoping she'll go away."

"Death-infested ruin?" Kevin Joe said. He looked at me.

"That's only the way she sees it," I said.

"Only me and the rest of the known world," Bina said.

"Bina," I said, looking her right in the eye, "shut the hell up or I'm gonna skin you now. This place is like heaven."

It was the second time that day I actually stood up to her.

Kevin Joe started smiling a little, looking away as if he didn't want us to see.

"Kevin Joe," I said. "I apologize for my friend. I would like to see the rest."

"Me, too," Bina sighed. "But Private Owen here wants some time alone with Charlie. Is that okay?"

"Sure," Kevin Joe said.

"Wait a minute," said Owen, about to resist.

"Owen, please?" Charlie said, and took his hand.

We left the two of them there and moved through the rest of the mansion. Kevin Joe showed us the dining room with its banquet length table, solid carved mahogany that had been gnawed, probably by the mangy dogs which roamed in and out of the house. Their hair and smell were everywhere.

In the kitchen, with its old hanging cast iron pots, its warped oak table and broken tile floor, we came upon an old woman. She sat with her back to us, her large, loose body spilling over a chair. She held a coffee cup in her hand.

"Kevin Joe," she said. "Is that you with some young folks?"

"Yes, mee-maw," he said quietly. "I've brought along some new friends from the state of Georgia. This is my daddy's mama, Miss Lila Glanville."

"What do they look like?" Miss Lila asked, her body twisting toward us. Her face tilted very far upward and the whites of her eyes were milked all the way across the color. We got too good a look at how badly she buttoned her own house-dress.

"All I get is blur, no matter what I do," she sighed. "Kevin Joe's my eyes."

Kevin Joe blushed a little. "Don't make me describe them, grandmaw," he whispered.

He hung his head even lower, his silky brown hair falling across his face. For all the filth of this place, he was immaculately clean. His clothes were fresh-looking and his hands were nice. He didn't look to me like someone struggling to maintain a house like this alone. He looked more genteel and sweet-natured than this place would suggest. And it was, I'm sure, politeness that made him reluctant to describe us.

Bina wore an old moth-eaten orange sweater and faded black sailor pants with a flap that buttoned along three sides of the square. Her wooden Dr. Scholl sandals were older than her underwear, which, thankfully, no one here had view of. The soles of the sandals were chipped and cracked and her long boney toes dangled unevenly over the edges of the front.

I was in what Bina called my stolen hippie clothes: mud-ruined blue jeans and a tie-dyed shirt my big sister Rachael wore to Woodstock. My hair was short because it never grew right, probably because, as a kid, I had a nervous habit of twisting clumps of it out with one hand while I sucked my thumb raw on the other.

"Who's this one here?" the old woman said, motioning with her crippled fingers toward me. "Is this one a girl? I think it's a girl."

Kevin Joe still hung his head and didn't answer.

"Well?" the old lady asked again.

"I'm a girl, Miss Lila," I said.

"What the hell am I?" Bina said.

"She only asked about me," I shrugged.

"Pretty?" Miss Lila persisted.

I wasn't sure which one of us she was talking about.

"I don't know," I said.

"Sure you do," she said. "A girl always knows if she's pretty."

"Valory's pretty," Bina said. "I'm not."

She was pretty, really, except that she didn't want to be. She had cheekbones like Katharine Hepburn and really nice honey-colored hair. But she washed her face with dish detergent, no lie, and pinned her hair back so tight that it made her eyes squint. I thought she was part Chinese when I first met her.

Kevin Joe moved closer to his grandmother and whispered something in her ear.

"I'm making them uncomfortable?" she repeated loudly. "How's that?"

The old woman heaved her body around in the chair, showing us her back again. "I'm just trying to talk to young folks you brought into my kitchen," she muttered. "If I'm rude, they don't have to be in here."

"I know it's still your house, mee-maw," Kevin Joe said. "But I'm the one keeps it up, best I can. I didn't mean to disturb you."

We had already begun to back out of the room.

"Lord preserve me from Family Hell," Bina whispered to me.

"Too late," I whispered back.

Later on, touring the bedrooms upstairs, Kevin Joe asked me, talking low, "Is your friend a homosexual?"

"Nah," I said, surprised at the thought. "She's just pissed off a lot."

Bina heard. She waited until Kevin moved away and then said, "Asshole."

I stopped walking. "Bina? What makes you happy?" I asked. I was wondering what she loved.

She looked sideways at me. "What kind of stupid question is that?"

"Joy," I said. "Do you have any?"

"Why the hell should I?" she said, looking surprised.

Kevin Joe had come back in search of us, and stood quietly in the doorway.

"I've refinished some mahogany crown molding in the second floor parlor," he said.

"Well how come you didn't fix the steps first?" Bina asked.

I shot her a look. "I'd like to see it," I said.

Bina stayed behind.

As we were heading across the hall, I asked Kevin Joe, "However will you know when you've got it right?"

He turned and looked at me, frowning. "Never thought about it," he said.

"What if you're reaching for something that might not even be there?"

"Like you mean this house may never be what I want it to?" Kevin Joe frowned.

"Like, could anything ever really turn out as perfect as it is in your head?" I said, knowing I was asking a different question than he thought.

He leaned against the wall, thinking. "Seems like I just have to push that worry aside," he said slowly. "Otherwise it would get in the way of the doing."

"You mean," I said, "some things you just shouldn't think about?"

"Way I see it," he nodded.

"My mom thinks that way," I said. "Back in '68, when my dad went MIA, she said, 'We just won't think like anything's different and he'll be home soon enough.'"

Kevin Joe frowned and reached out for my hand. "Hell," he said. "I'm sorry."

I liked the way his hand felt around mine, a little rough and callused from the work, but nice, too.

"I'm sorry too," I said. "especially 'cause it didn't work, you know?"

"Are you two kissin' in there?" Bina yelled.

Kevin Joe looked embarrassed again.

"We'd better go," I said.

The whole time we had been upstairs, downstairs Charlie had been doing a different kind of rebuilding. While we were touring the house and they were alone in that ballroom, Charlotte managed to patch herself and Owen back together.

"He's my fiancé again," she smiled.

Owen gave her a one-armed hug and looked at us with embarrassment. "I was just being an idiot," he said.

I looked sharply at Bina to be sure she wouldn't make a crack.

"We'll try to do it by April," Charlie said.

"What about your German?" Bina hissed. "What about the Embassy?"

Charlie shrugged. "I could still," she said. "I probably could."

"How disgusting can you get," Bina said to her. "How stupid can you be?"

"Bina you are just plain mean," I said. "What gives you the right?"

"I can see my talents are wasted here," she muttered.

"What talents?" I said. "You're like a rainstorm at a picnic."

"It's okay, Valory," Charlie said. "I'm happy as I ever could be."

Bina looked thunderstruck and didn't talk again.

To celebrate their reconciliation, Owen offered to take us all to a drive-in movie.

Kevin Joe couldn't go and I felt disappointed.

"I'll drive you all back," he said. "but I've got work to do here before I lose the whole weekend."

As we walked to the car, I dropped back to talk to him alone.

"Listen," I said to him. "Can I write to you or something?"

"Well, sure," he said. "That would be nice."

So I wrote out my address and took down his and made him promise that he'd answer my letters.

Back on post, Owen got busy rounding up some guys for the drive-in. The three of us girls sat outside on a bench, waiting. We were starved and Owen got us some peanut butter crackers from a vending machine. We were sharing them between us.

"I'm sorry, Charlie," Bina said. "I guess I've treated you wrong."

Charlie nodded. "You have," she said. "But that's all right. I know you mean to protect me."

Even though Bina glanced over at me, waiting, I felt no call to add anything. It seemed like something between the two of them.

Owen set us up with two guys from his barracks for some kind of triple date to see "The Way We Were." For Bina, there was an unsuspecting schmoe called Norman. For no reason I could figure out, he had scabs on his nose and forehead. The only thing he had going for him, and I'm sure this is what got him invited, was that he owned a 1960 Chevy Nomad, one of those great old station wagons, the last of the wing-fins. You could see how he loved that car. It was a gleaming machine, polished black with shining white-wall wheels. The chrome was mirror-like, even up on the roof rack. He opened the car doors with a chamois cloth.

"It keeps the handles from smudging," he said.

After a dark glance at me, Bina sat up front with him. Charlie and Owen cuddled in the back seat. That left the cargo space for me and my date, a husky farmboy named Dean. He had a face sprayed with freckles, which combined with his dumb expression made him look something like an Ayrshire heifer. I could tell by how much cologne he wore that he thought he was going to get somewhere with me. So, I spent most of the night lying on my stomach in the back of the Nomad, protecting my most vital private parts from his freckled hands, watching Robert Redford up on screen being good-looking even while going by the name of Hubbell. And all night, Dean kept getting on my nerves.

"Look," I said, peeling his thick fingers out from under my shirt for the third time. "I know you're thinking we're gonna have sex, or at the very least that I'm gonna help you have sex alone. But it's not gonna happen."

"Why the hell not?" Dean said. "You don't know me. I don't know you. We're never gonna see each other again. What's the risk?"

"The risk?" I repeated, thinking of my dad's Smith & Wesson. "You have no idea."

I didn't bother telling him, but for me, there was T-Bone to consider. I loved him. And already today I promised to write letters to another guy. So I needed to stick with my code, to keep my sex with other people on the up and up and not do it for jokes. I had to draw the line somewhere. Bina kept glancing back at me. Finally, she turned around in her seat and started to climb over. First she climbed onto the back seat, jostling Charlie and Owen who were locked together, kissing. Then she climbed over the seat into the back, wedging herself between me and the wheel well on the passenger side.

"I want to tell you something about today," she said.

Dean had slipped his hand onto my backside, and as I turned to knock it off, Bina reached over and pinched the skin on the back of his arm hard.

"Hey!" he yelled.

"Well leave her the hell alone and watch the movie," Bina said. "We're talking here."

She turned back to me. "Remember what you said today about me just being pissed off?"

"Yeah," I said. "So?"

"Well what if that's not all it is?" She paused a minute. The light from the movie kept changing the colors of her face. "What if I am? What he said?"

"Oh," I said.

She needed me to say something much more important to her than that and I didn't know what to say.

"Well, I think you'll be okay, Jobina," I said.

I had absolutely no idea what I meant by that.

"My family doesn't want me around," she said. "I'm reviled through the Bible Belt. You and Charlie are all I've got. And I've been awful to you."

"That part is true," I said.

"I need to find a way to be happy as who I am," she said. "Your question made me realize that today."

The funny thing is, as hard as I knew it was for her to tell me the truth, it was the first time I ever heard anything in Bina's voice that sounded alive.

"You're okay with this?" she asked.

I nodded. "Sure," I said. "Why not?" I can't cast any stones. Wouldn't if I could.

She hugged me. "Thanks," she said, getting ready to climb back.

"Don't go yet," I told her. "There's something else."

I picked a secret that wouldn't scare her off. Still, it was hard to say it, because my mom had made us promise. "It's not true," she kept saying. And as long as Rachael and I pretended right along with her, then it couldn't come true. But I felt the words down there, starting to come up from inside me for the first time.

"My daddy's dead," I whispered.

Bina grabbed my arm. "What?"

"The army moved him from missing to declared. But there's no body. We don't have any proof. They just say so."

"When?" she asked.

"Last week," I told her. "My mom refused to go to the memorial service. She says that's giving up hope."

And as soon as I said it, I realized.

"That's it," I said, suddenly knowing.

"What?" Bina asked.

We love whatever gives us hope.

"Bina, I'm not going back with you," I said.

"What?" she said again, "I think I heard you wrong."

"I'm stayin'," I said. "Right here in Columbia."

I already knew all about the hope of love. So did my mother and Charlie. And for that matter, so did the characters up there on the screen. But I didn't know the kind of hope that T-Bone was talking about. Or the kind, maybe, my father had, believing he could change the world. Or Kevin Joe's kind, believing he could change it back.

All night long, my thoughts had been rising away from everybody in the car toward Spanish moss and patches of dust, cold marble and old mahogany, toward everything I never knew and always wanted, and all I really wanted to do was find Kevin Joe. I wanted to be back in that run down mansion with that clean, shy boy and his nearly-blind grandmother. I wanted to help him fix that house up—a lot of paint, and clearing away—getting the dog smell out of the kitchen. I wanted to be another set of eyes for Miss Lila Glanville. I could tell her everything I saw, and she would see it all over again, just like it was brand new washed clean of all the sorrow and loss and ruin and heartbreak. I wanted, more than anything, to share a new dream. To make things the way they were. Or maybe, the way they could be. I'm not really sure. But these stirrings were a recognition of love as strong as I had ever known it, of deep longing for something that promised to stand forever, or nearly forever, in the face of threat, weaponry, and devastation.

So, I would find a job somewhere and help Kevin Joe. It wasn't like finding my own dream, I know. But it would get me close enough so that I might learn where a dream like that would take me.

"What about school?" Bina asked me.

I'd lose a month, or a semester. Maybe I wouldn't go back at all. And Charlie'd lose the embassy job. Bina would lose her family.

"I think we've all gone crazy," she said. Her first professional opinion.

So there we were, the three of us girls, barely adults, our weekend only half-way done and everyone of us at a crossroads.

On screen, Streisand was handing out pamphlets, hoping to convince people of the truth as she saw it. But they hurried by, huddled into their own lives, paying no attention.

That was years ago, now. And it turns out, we can never really know why we love what we love or where our hopes will take us. But inside that gleaming Nomad on that night in Columbia, when a blanket of quiet settled over everything and everyone, I remember it felt as if each of us in our own private way sensed something was nearing an end. But after all this time, who knows what's really true? Anybody else might say that's just my way of remembering. And I wouldn't ever try to tell them they were wrong.

A Fire Goeth Before Him

M Y SON IS CALLED AMMON. It means *The Hidden*. I choose this name as soon as I know that I'm carrying him again, that he has returned to my womb. As soon as I know, I shield him, the knowledge of him, from the others, from the ones who'd do him harm, from the ones who would remove him again.

His father is Nathan, whose name means *Endowed with the Gift of Prophecy*. He does not deserve this name, because he doesn't know the future. He doesn't know this boy will be born, so this son will be mine alone. Nathan thinks it ended with a business deal: a fattened check and a Porsche Carrera in exchange for a vacuumed womb. But Nathan couldn't stay away from me, could never stay away from me, and so the baby returned.

I have found someone to be my husband. His name is Samuel. I check before I marry him, and believe it should be fine, because Samuel means *Asked of God*. We have a deal: I give him Nathan's money and follow him to his boyhood town where he promises us a home. I become his wife. But he doesn't know a thing about me.

Nathan stalks through my dreams. I squander my sleep to watch for what he finds. One night, he sat quite still, astonishingly still, in a large scarlet chair. A voice came from his forehead that said, "I am the man." I stood before him with Ammon's shoe in my right hand. It glowed with a strange light. I could not wake up.

SOMETHING GROWS WITHIN ME each day. I suspect it's a power I have yet to harness. On the telephone with cousin Rachael, I hear myself say, "It's a psychic transmission. I turn the television on with my mind." I didn't mean to let it slip.

"How long does this have to go on?" she asks. "Are you getting help?"

She knows more about me than is safe. I worry she and Valory will take me away before my work is done.

So I say, "I'm seeing someone." I don't say who.

"How often?" she asks.

"Every week," I say. I see people every week.

On the day of my marriage, Nathan sends roses. His note says, "It's a smaller pond, Marlena. Splash softly."

I am Marlena: *Exalted by the Lord who forgives her sins.* So I know I am forgiven on the day of the marriage as I stuff my wedding suit inside the chimney and wear black velvet that plunges low to uncover the swelling of my vein-slashed breasts. All those years with Nathan in my bed never made me good enough, never made the child good enough. The child was not good enough because half of him was me. I say Ammon is good enough. I say Nathan had no right.

On the honeymoon, I practice my new power. Sam watches me as I sit on the floor before the darkened TV screen. He passes by me on his way out the door, but he doesn't ask questions. I continue my work, and am elated when the television snaps on after only a few hours concentration. The program is not one I recognized, but there is something familiar about the people. I watch for a while before turning it off with a nod of my head. Sam has left the hotel for a swim. Throughout all the days we're there, I never let him touch any part of my body.

THE HOUSE Samuel spent my money on is not as he promised. There are mice in the cupboards. When they die, their bodies stiffen and their heads curl forward on their necks, with their mouths open slightly, to expose the tiny points of their front teeth.

I walk room to room and echoes follow me. I touch dying vegetation that pushes up between the floorboards of the kitchen. It withers in my hands. The plaster dust that hangs thick in the air clouds my sight and makes me wheeze. I step over scattered pieces of walls and ceiling that the carpenters have brought down, which no longer shield me from the outside world. Rain comes through the opened roof, air whistles through the torn up walls. Sam's carpenters claim to be fixing everything at once, but nothing seems fixable. On and on, vast areas are demolished with an arsenal of ballpeens and hatchets.

Through autumn I can do no more than lie damp and weak with chills on a sofa covered in drop cloths. I have no bedroom; the upstairs rooms have been torn apart for rebuilding. There is nowhere to be alone. I close my eyes to shut out the workmen moving around me, to deafen myself to the noises of their hammers and saws and radios. The child inside me twists into deeper recesses of my body, curling into himself. It feels like the power growing within me, but I can't tell any longer if the power which grows is mine, or if the power is not mine. If the power isn't mine, I'm in peril, and the strength of this twisting bodes badly, and warns me of jeopardy. I worry that this child is not returning for love, but for revenge.

I am alone to face this fear. Sam spends weeks away from this demolition, camped at waste sites, citing hazards to the general population for local newspapers. He phones with excuses for staying away. But the excuses just remind me what the deal is: I buy him this house in exchange for the marriage. But I never expect to be left so completely alone so fast.

Sam's peculiar kind of life thrives in the air of a science lab. Human experience is filtered through the grids of advanced degrees in environmental knowledge. He is trained to measure evil through gauges and scopes.

"You will never see a flaming devil with your own eyes!" I scream at him on the phone.

I have no one.

My brother Martin might have helped me, but he's freshly dead from drinking and upending tables at roadhouses. Sometimes he'd drive hours beyond the closest bars just to find some place where he never smashed tables or insulted the bartenders. He called this "Raising New Hell." This last time, someone turned the table on him, and his head was split as it hit the parking lot after that someone, we don't know who, drove a fist through his left eye and sent him down.

My sister, Miranda, would have clung to Martin's casket and cried. She'd have pretended to remember his good qualities as we watched the casket being lowered into the ground. But she's heroin-dead, battling her will to live for years, and finally laying, a victorious corpse, in the bathroom of a Pump N Go off Route 1 in Swainsboro. That was last year, on her twentieth birthday, the week before my wedding.

Martin and I made her arrangements, but I alone make Martin's. Before his casket is closed for the viewing, I insist on seeing his smashed face in private. I stare into his shattered eye, and remove the dagger from my purse.

"See this?" I ask him.

He should remember it. It was the dagger he used to use on us, his two sisters, when we were too small to defend ourselves. He'll want it now, I'm sure.

I am careful about the design I make on his forehead. His flesh doesn't cut the way I expect. It opens like a piece of fruit that has rotted, then dried. Even when I slide the blade into his cheek, nothing fluid seeps out. The handle stands upright easily enough, that much is good. It extends from his face like a pearl-colored bone, growing free from his death, growing in a heavenly direction. It is my prayer, and when I close the lid, I feel the snap of *forever, amen.*

At the funeral, cousins Rachael and Valory are the only family to come. They stand beside me and support my elbows when I have to waddle over the soft, opened ground. Rachael has classes to teach in New Orleans, and leaves the next morning. But Valory stays with me through the days after Sam goes away again. It's good, having her here, but it's hard too, her knowing me as well as she does and watching me so closely. I can't practice the power.

Late at night, we sit in our pajamas, not having to talk too much to explain ourselves. Crickets sing from beneath the piles of wood in the livingroom. Stars shine through parts of the ceiling where the tarp blows open, and leaves float down into the room. Like camping.

"It's awful here, isn't it?" I say, looking around at the destruction of the rooms.

"You want permission to hate it?" Valory says, always knowing somehow. "Go ahead and hate it all. It sucks."

In the daytime, she takes charge of the carpenters for me, going over their projected plans for the rest of the job. Making decisions and choices, checking their supplies against their bills.

"I told them they better get their damn jobs out of the way before winter sets in. Otherwise you and this kid will be freezing to death."

I can't even thank her. I just cry. I cry because those bastards stand and listen to her. I cry because I look like a cow and they snicker behind my back. I stopped trying to speak with them weeks ago. Now, I hide from them through most of the day. Since there is no kitchen, I have to eat my meals out of the house. Sometimes, because I don't know this town very well and don't know where to go, I leave and sneak down into the old root cellar, sitting there for hours on the dank, dirt floor, until the noises and footsteps above me stop and I know they are gone for the day. I don't say anything about this to Valory, because while she's there, I don't need to hide.

She stays for a few days, helping to clean up some of the mess. Sweeping plaster dust and paint chips, she begins to curse under her breath. "You shouldn't be breathing this shit. It's poison. Mr. Almighty Environment isn't here to breathe it in, is he?"

She wants me to leave with her.

"Don't decide anything permanent right now. Tell Sam you're staying with me until the house is livable. That'll take a few months. It'll buy you some time."

I'm afraid. What if I go and he won't want me back? Ammon will have no home.

"All my money is tied up in this house," I say.

"You told me that before this ridiculous wedding. But you don't mean ALL of the money from Nate, too?"

She's the only one who knows about the Goodbye and Good Riddance check Nate presented to me after the abortion. Before the baby came back.

I'm not listening to her. I'm worried about the power. If I leave with her, I'll never be able to practice. I have to make myself strong, to protect Ammon. Mothers should do that.

"Valory, I'll be fine," I say, watching as a blue jay flies through an opening in the livingroom wall. It lands on a pile of carpentry tools.

"You're so NOT fine," Valory says. "I don't know where to start."

The bird lifts its tail and deposits his shit on a planing tool.

"You're sick. You're alone. And," Valory sweeps her hand to indicate the surroundings, "you're losing your mind in West Bumblefuck, Virginia."

"It's really sort of wonderful," I say, "being at the center of all this activity."

"I have a shoot in Baltimore in three days," she says. "At least come with me for that. I can comp the whole thing."

I just shake my head. So, a few days later, she's packed and heading off.

"I'll call you Wednesday unless I hear from you first," she says, scribbling a list of numbers—car phone, hotel, agency.

I stuff the numbers into my bra, feeling the scratch of the paper soften as it absorbs my sweat, imagining the numbers running against each other, turning fluid and seeping into my skin.

"I'm fine," I smile.

"You're full of shit," she says, hugging me hard. "But I love you."

I don't answer. I love her so much I can't stand it anymore. I want her to just go away.

ONCE I'M ALONE AGAIN, the TV begins to go on without my willing it to. That is, the will is not consciously directed. The first time this happened, the screen lightened slowly on a young girl. Her hair was dirty as swampsludge. She was playing in a kind of woods, something between a wooded lot and a small glen. Her knees were scabbed, or scarred, I couldn't see which, and she ran. That's all she did. She ran through the weeds and the bugs and she flapped her arms and hooted as she went. The word she hooted was "Ro-nee, Ro-nee" like a birdcall. I watched and knew that somewhere in the woods her brother hid, waiting with his pearl-handled knife to hurt her if she blundered too close. She knew this, too, knew all his hiding places and pretended not to, so that he wouldn't find new ones. Her brother was violent, but stupid. For this, the girl loved her brother and was grateful. She understood it was easier when violence and stupidity went together.

AMMON IS BORN. On the day of his birth, there are special forecasts of weather never before seen. Storms of great magnitude are predicted, with sun blazes that will ignite the trees. But this child is born instead, and so the world is saved.

THE POWER IS STILL MINE. On the morning of my first dawn with Ammon, I lay him sleeping in his crib and move carefully down the stairs. The TV screen is lit and that same little girl is there, asleep in her room. The wind moved the curtains so that they filled with air slowly puffing out like the chest of a singer. Then they gave a little flap and the air rushed out beneath them. A man in a dark blue bathrobe entered the room quietly and stood over the little girl. The curtains puffed and lowered, puffed and lowered behind her. The man raised his fist and brought it down hard on the little girl's back. Over and over again, he brought down his fist. I wondered if the little girl was dead, because she never moved. Not once. The man finally stopped his fist, as it waited high in the air. This time, when he brought it down, it was to straighten and smooth the coverlet over the little girl's form, which remained motionless in the bed. Then the man tucked the hand into the pocket of his robe, tucked the hand as if he was concealing a weapon. He stumbled from the room.

THE PAIN OF NOT-GETTING comes from need. This is what I know. To teach Ammon not to need is to save him.

Happy shall he be, that taketh and dasheth the little ones against the stones, the Bible says. And so I know that I should dash my son against the stone of not-getting to free him from want and hunger. This duty tears at me, and when his eyes look toward me I see their earnestness, feel his need in a way that makes me want to care. But I stop myself. I harden my eyes when I look at him. This change happens: his face slackens, then his eyes wander away from my face and back, away and back, as if searching for something to fill his need and, finding nothing, return each time to me, in hope, then look away again with no hope.

"Hope is an illusion," I say to him. "Be free of it."

I know we will have to perform this exercise again and again before the final outcome. But one day, I know, the light behind his eyes will dim, and in that way I will know when we have reached the death of his expectation. In that way, I will make him invulnerable.

Sam's mother has a key made. She comes in at all hours. Sometimes she is in the kitchen with coffee made when I wake at 6 a.m. Sometimes she is with Ammon, rocking him, feeding him.

"I hope you don't mind," she says. "I'm just trying to give you some rest."

I have a very good smile for times like these. I tilt my head gently and make my eyes look loving before letting my lips curve slowly.

"You worry too much about me, Mother Rawlins," I say. "I feel wonderful."

She smiles back at me from the rocking chair. But I know she suspects, and she is out to spoil everything.

One morning I sit in the living room, naked, waiting for her. I plan to spring like a cat when she opens the door and frighten her near to death. I wonder, will she dare tell Sam? But I fall asleep waiting, there on the rug. When I wake up, the room is flooded with sunlight, the child's screams are ringing through the house, and the plumber is standing over me, smirking.

I WON'T LET ANYTHING interfere with my goals. I sit practicing until the bones behind my eyebrows start to ache. Sometimes I feel the world turning because behind my eyes my mind plays tricks and I begin to believe I am not myself. Other times the screen will light quickly, and I see her again, walking like a dream through an empty house.

Her hair is still stringy and unwashed. She is motherless, and keeps many secrets. She keeps the secret of food smuggled and hidden beneath her bed, the secret of children's sins for which she fears she lost her mother, of cries swallowed down and compacted by the taste of pillow in the night, of flesh from purple to yellow.

I want sleep. I want strength. I try to sleep through distractions. Sam is gone again.

Nathan finds me, and I suspect Valory. As if what he tells me doesn't matter at all, he says, "Maybe I'll drive to that outpost of yours, just to see what you'd do."

That's how I know he's learned about my baby.

"You can't come," I say.

"Why?"

Because you can't see Ammon, because he is not ready, is what I can't say.

"Because you didn't want me," is what I say instead. "Because you broke my heart."

"Break your heart," he corrects me. "I break your heart, over and over again, just as you love me to do. And I am coming, Marlena, because its time for me to do it again."

What he says stops my speech, so I hang up the phone and try to breathe.

"I don't love him," I say to Ammon. "I love the TV."

Of course, it's not the TV itself; it's the light of the screen that I love. Once, spying on Ronnie, who was my mother, I watched her dance all alone, that flickering blue TV light lifting her face and form, turning it heavenly. That's what I love: the wash of that blue light as it dances over me. It's all that's left of my memory—that hollow light where my mother no longer dances.

Sam who had promised to be my husband is still gone. Always gone. Nathan calls again.

"I want to see the boy," he says.

"You have no right," I say. Our exercises are not finished. Ammon is not yet invincible. It is not time.

"One look at that child will tell me if I have the right," he says.

I hang up the phone quickly and wander the rooms, talking out loud to the torn down walls. "What can I do? How can I stop this?" I have to work faster to make Ammon strong. I have to practice my own power, to control the forces around us. Nathan is getting closer. I am afraid. Ammon's eyes follow me as I pace.

Then, yesterday, as I practice my power, my head begins to ache with the effort and I go upstairs to sleep. Ammon is crying. A strange sense draws me to his room. The whole place is ablaze, including the crib. I run through the fire to where the baby lay. His blankets are dissolving in flame. His skin is singeing. He looks up at me, and smiles.

SAM SAYS THEY FOUND ME in the diningroom, unconscious, and that I never could have been in the baby's room at all. The firemen think smoked caused my blackout. I don't care what any of them think. I know it was the shock of the burning baby's smile that caused me to collapse. That was when I realized that he was already stronger than the exercises, stronger than anything I had planned. It frightened me at first, and I ran.

Insurance men say the fire started in the walls. They blame the carpenters' heat gun and old wood. A deadly combination, they say. Sam believes this. But it's not true. What's true is that the fire started inside the baby. He is my child. This is his gift. He is the boy who burns.

Ammon will survive. He must. He is the teacher, and he has taught me truth. The fire was his way to purify himself. I was not needed. Nor was Nathan, who can't touch him anymore, even if he still wanted to.

Nathan will leave us alone now. Ammon no longer has the skin, the face, the hair of his father. He has, in his own way, in his own time, shed them to be wholly himself, and in that way, wholly mine. For us, he has traveled to the end of the fiery death which was no death, and has returned to me. That is what his smile told me. It said *Now we can forgive each other. We can be mother and child without end, in perfect love, amen.*

This is what I say to him now, through the glass. I wait until the nurses have turned away and whisper to him in his captivity: "*A fire goeth before him, and burneth up his enemies round about.*"

I wait, watching. His little arms become still within the bandaging. His head can't move, but his eyes find mine, blazing. I nod, holding him in my gaze. I need no longer let him fall. Soon we will be free, together, alone.

"*His lightnings enlightened the world*," I say.

He nods his tiny bandaged head to tell me: *The earth sees, and trembles.*

Some of the T-Bone Stories

ONE THING I LIKED about Tommy Bones was that he never left for good. No matter what either of us said or did, he'd be hanging around soon enough, waiting for me again. Sometimes the two of us roamed the Fort Bragg housing areas, which was where we lived. Sometimes we snuck our bikes to the highway, heading out to ride the farm roads in the dark, stealing corn in the middle of the night, or climbing the rolling water sprayers that stretched like enormous insects across the fields.

Tommy Buonorotti was his real name. But the other fosters called him Tommy Bones because, even as a baby, he was skinny as a chicken, his rib cage pushing through his skin, and the wing bones of his back jutting out at angles behind him. Mrs. Robart, the lady who took him in, hated all her fosters. Most times she locked them out of the house and sat on a folding lawn chair in the empty livingroom, drinking beer and cursing into the air. The kids prowled the streets 'til all hours, half-dressed and hungry, with dirty nails and snotty faces, running fevers and coughing mucus.

I was glad about them being there, since they were the only ones in the neighborhood more sorry-looking than me. For some reason in early babyhood, I'd taken to yanking out patches of my own hair. There were small bald spots all over

147

my head. The rest of my hair was thin and scraggly and my sister Rachael cut it every few days with our mom's sewing scissors to stop me getting a good grip, so it barely reached my ears and stuck out in every direction on my head.

"Midget, I swear," she'd say, every time she'd find more hair on my pillow. "If you don't quit this, I'm gonna spread Vaseline on your head."

I secretly ate a hunk of Vaseline every time she said it, trying to empty the jar before she could make good on her threat.

As kids, Tommy and I didn't care if we were a raggedy match. We were just hooked up, with him wilder and me smarter—him thinking up the things to dare and me planning them, or getting us out of the trouble we were in if we got caught.

As grownups, sometimes we were still in that place, with him dishing up fantasies and me pushing them into action. Something about him kept me giddy and confused, like I didn't know who wanted what or what the hell I was doing. But I usually didn't care. I didn't even care this time, when our plans meant I had to take off on my husband Kevin Joe in the middle of the night. Kev and I'd been married three years and I'd taken off a dozen times before. This time, I was going with Tommy because we had a special thing in mind.

BUT BEING TOGETHER for more than one day straight was always hard on Tommy and me. By the second or third night out, he was chain-blowing joints and I was gulping bourbon at a wobbly table in the Hazy Day Club. He was up there wailing on mouth harp, fronting a Delta blues band. I was hoping a few more shots of Echo Spring would clear out the wheeze in my chest, knowing how he wouldn't want me to leave while he was on stage, no matter how much the cigarette smoke kicked up my asthma. I didn't mind so much. I loved watching him. He grew up to look fine, in his own way. He'd bench pressed his childhood skinniness into a little bit of bulk—and he was a powerful mover when his mouth harp rhythm took over. Earlier that night, I watched him dress for this gig. He slipped into a plain black tee-shirt, pretending he wasn't showing off for me. Then he angled his old beret, as a joke he was serious about, over the scar to the right of his hairline. He smiled his crooked smile to himself every time he checked me still watching him.

"You gonna be my playbaby tonight?" he squinted his eyes at me. "Playbaby" was his way of saying, "Nobody get nervous; it's not for real."

He never wanted anything to be for real. It was another thing I liked about him, even though it sometimes backfired on me—like with him acting like the whole month of June fell off this year's calendar just because, after all these years, we finally consummated whatever we are together, right there on his rug, on the night of the 10th. I waited my whole life to be with him like that. But you'd think I'd tricked him into it, the way he acted. Like I had hit him in the back of the head when he wasn't looking and dragged his pants off.

"What the hell happened here?" he said. We were still tangled together, and suddenly he's pretending he just walked in.

"You want me to explain it to you?"

"I don't want you to say anything," he said. "Not one word."

He yanked his clothes free of mine, and pulled them back around himself. He slid away from me, toward the steps.

"You can sleep down here, if you want," he said.

I lay in a heap on the floor, still exposed in all kinds of places that no longer felt safe, now that the air had changed.

He pulled himself slowly to standing and looked down at me like we'd never formally met.

"Goodnight," he said, sounding strangled.

"T-Bone, please," I said.

He stood there in the shadow without talking.

"Tommy Bones, god damn it, don't do this to me." I could tell by his breathing that he had started to cry. We were both crying.

"It can't be this way, Midgy," he said. "I keep telling you. If I start doing that, I'll start doin' it all—that's what you never get."

"I don't believe you," I said.

"I can't help it," he answered.

Then he went on the road the very next day without so much as a nod toward me, still sleeping there on the floor, and by the time he came home, he acted like nothing new had happened between us. By then I figured who needs conversation. I knew the way it was and just how much I could count on.

Then last night, at the end of the last set, he started in with his talking again.

"If you ever acted like it was fine with you," he said, "I'd be on you like a fly on shit."

"Flatterer," I smirked.

"In a New York minute," he kept up, "like a flash."

I figured, okay, I'll ride this horse again. "T-Bone," I said slowly, running my finger through a puddle on the bar, "how do you keep forgetting it is fine with me?"

He stood so fast that his stool fell over, but he didn't bother with it. "Valory Midget Meade, it'll never be fine with you. Trust me on that," he said, and walked away.

So I went right back to feeling guarded, knowing no matter what it seemed, this was where it stayed. Except that I was on the road with him—that was something different—and we were headed for Fayetteville.

It's a wooden apple, I kept telling myself, stimulating simulation, but I didn't know what to believe, exactly. It was possible that all the years we spent together brought us beyond romance and consummation. Maybe our history joined us together in a kind of asexual psychotic oneness that was all the love anybody could expect. At least, that's what I thought as I watched the lights of the stage turn T-Bone's hair gold, then green, any color but what it really was. I sat thinking back to Kevin Joe, and felt sorry to be leaving him again. I wondered if he knew I was gone.

T-Bone always said, "When I leave a woman, she stays left." I guess that's true. In the last three years he's left twelve or fifteen for dead, believing it's better than leaving the same person over and over again, like I do.

His last one was a waitress named Honey. Last time I saw her was April when I went over his house to pick up the Harley—it's a '42 Flathead he taught me to ride years ago, as a kind of wedding gift.

"You learn how to tank shift and it's yours," he said, "as long as you store it here."

I saw he wanted that Flathead to be a solid connection, to give me a reason to keep showing up anytime. It was a sign that he forgave me marrying Kev, and that he wanted forgiveness for not stopping me. It seemed really sweet to me.

"Got yourself a deal," I said, kissing him on the cheek. I knew better than to tell him I understood. I just risked my neck learning to tank shift, to give him the message in a way he could appreciate.

Anyway, this day in April T-Bone wasn't there. As I opened the garage, Honey walked around from the side of the house, her face a little swollen and puffy. She was wearing one of T-

Bone's jackets. Its arms hung below her finger tips, and she had her own arms wrapped around herself, like it was a black leather straightjacket, like she couldn't stay in one piece without the extra tightness. And this was only after a few weeks of living there.

"T-Bone's gone," she said. "I don't think he's coming back any time soon."

"Jesus," I said. "You look like hell."

"I look like hell all the time now," Honey nodded, looking away. I knew she was ashamed, but knew, too, that she wanted me to see. Why else would she have come around to the driveway?

"I keep doin' things wrong," Honey said. "There are so many god-damned rules he springs on me from nowhere. I can't answer the phone, I can't use the towels on the bathroom racks, I can't sort the mail. I can't spray perfume on myself anywhere but in the bathroom."

"Don't ever put something in the waste cans, except the one in the kitchen with the lid," I nodded. "In case you don't know that one."

"He hasn't talked to me in days," Honey said, turning to swipe at her nose, "because I put some old albums back on the wrong shelf." She ran her fingers through her matted hair, wincing. "What made him extra mad," she said, "was the covers pointing in the wrong direction."

I knew this pattern. It wouldn't be long now before she was gone. Right now, she was still believing there was some way she could get in, something she could learn that would help her connect. But I knew Tommy'd keep changing the rules, that he'd allow no connecting, ever. That's what kept me afloat through all of his entanglements—the knowledge that he could never let them outlive a good virus.

He was sure to be at Belly's now, drinking breakfast; I wondered if I should cruise by, just to sit with him awhile.

"He won't be back for a few days," I told her, swinging my leg over the seat. "Then he'll show up with at least three friends, a woman he won't introduce, and a case of beer."

Honey watched me yank the shift into reverse. "You love him, don't you?" she said.

"Sure," I said. "That's why I live somewhere else."

BUT HERE WE WERE together, on the road, on the last night of his gig. We packed up the equipment and sent the band on without him. Then we headed down the farm roads to the Army post without ever saying anything to each other about how long we planned to stay. We got to where we were going in a few hours time, and pulled into our old development around 4:00 a.m., careful not to keep our headlights on as we parked the car.

"Good thing there's still enough dark," T-Bone said, pulling our blankets, flashlights and provisions out of his trunk. He trundled most of it in his big arms, giving me only a small flashlight to aim at our feet. But it wasn't like we needed it. There are things that your nervous system never forgets, it's stored in your wiring forever. And walking this route to the back of my old house was one of those things. Never mind we were on military property, sneaking across the hallowed land of officers' homes. T-Bone and I spent many an all-nighter wandering exactly where we were headed now, wandering all over government bluegrass. Soon, we were in my old back-yard, kneeling in the farthest corner of the lot, where a jutting rock that thrust itself up from the ground concealed the handle of a fall-out shelter my paranoid father installed without official permission all those years before.

"No way it's gonna open after all this time," T-Bone said, yanking at the rock.

I edged myself in front and took the rock firmly between my hands. I even remembered its roughness against my palms as if it were just the other day. Just one slow pull out, then down, and the sod-covered door popped open with the sound of a vacuum seal.

"Sweet Jesus Divine," Tommy said, shining his flashlight into the cavern below. "I do believe we're home."

The scent of the air outside had shifted and the earliest birds were starting their titter in the trees.

"Let's get down there before somebody wakes up," I said, giving him a little push with my shoulder.

We both climbed through the opening, and I pulled the door closed behind us. There was no sense in thinking our eyes would adjust to this darkness, so we groped around the way we used to when we were kids until we found the generator switch. A dim, golden light glowed with a humming sound, illuminating the space, which was exactly as we had left it, ten years before.

"Ha-ha," T-Bone hooted, "still smells like the inside of a tuna can," he said, putting his arm around me and hugging unusually tight.

"Happy anniversary, Tommy Bones," I said, kissing his cheek.

"Happy anniversary, Midget Meade," he said, squeezing tighter.

We'd planned this celebration ten years before, even left food behind that we imagined our future selves would want to celebrate with.

"Shall we?" I said. The can of Charlie's Chips sat right in the center of a card table, behind two quarts of Schmidt's Beer.

"Shit yeah," T-Bone said, pulling an old bottle opener off the shelf, and popping the bottlecap off the Schmidt's. He handed me the bottle.

"You first, Midge," he said.

"To us," I said, taking a huge gulp and swallowing slowly, letting a thin stream of bitter warmth trickle down my throat as my eyes teared over.

Tommy wrapped his fingers around mine and held the bottle to his lips. He drank long and deep, holding his head back and closing his eyes.

"Ahh," he swallowed, looking around.

"Don't you dare start cleaning anything," I warned him.

"Just this," he said, squatting to pick up an argyle sock twisted on the floor. He dangled it at the tips of his fingers, "Memento," he said, the hurt slipping across his eyes, and then away. "That old dead bitch," he said. "You saved my tail that time."

"Like there ever was any question," I said.

BACK WHEN TOMMY was fourteen, Mrs. Robart died of a stroke. None of the kids said a thing to anyone. They left her body where it fell and argued among themselves for days over what to do. Finally, her fat sister discovered the corpse and all hell broke loose, with kids running away in all directions. A social worker placed a few remaining kids with a new family in Selbyville. But Tommy was the hardest case because of poor behavior and bad health, and because standardized tests showed a lower than average IQ. It looked like he was heading back to the foster home.

There was no question that he would hide in the shelter. It had been our secret place for years. He just slipped in for a three-week stay, and I smuggled him down a suitcase of essentials: Mallo Cups, Twinkies, Ovaltine (which he liked to eat right out of the jar) and some of my father's wool socks and sweaters, a ski mask and Chiclets.

"The socks and sweaters are too big," he said.

"You spent your whole life wearing other people's clothes," I said, "Why complain now?"

"I never wore a dead guy's before," he said.

"He's only missing. Roll them and stuff them, don't think about it," I said. "And by the way, you're welcome."

My sister Rachael was in art school by then. Nobody noticed me missing. Still I was careful to leave only when my mother watched "The Edge of Night," and again each night when she slept. Those were the times I slipped into the shelter and spent the best hours of my day with Tommy. We played Clue and Concentration, and listened to my transistor radio.

A few times, I even risked sleeping there with him, both of us nestled, fully dressed, into surplus issue blankets so scratchy that just turning in your sleep would wake you up. But that was only on the nights my mother hit the Seconal harder than usual. Then, it was sure she'd be down 'til lunch the next day.

I told Tommy that my mother and I would have to relocate if my father was moved from MIA to Officially Deceased. Tommy said he was planning on leaving soon too, thumbing it south to someplace like Florida or Mexico.

"You probably wouldn't come with me," he said.

He knew damn well there was never any place I wanted to be except with him, that I would've followed if there was a way.

"You know I count her pills," I said. "If I'm not here, there's nobody to hide them."

"She's gonna die sometime, Midge," he said, "right?"

I shrugged.

"The answer's yes," he said.

"So?"

"So, we'll give her ten years to OD," he said. "Then we'll meet right back here. When we're twenty-four. Right here."

I burst into tears. "You're being awful!" I yelled. "How could you leave me alone for ten years!"

That's when I made him promise he'd never go completely. He promised to call from the road, or wherever he was. I even smuggled him down a tobacco can filled with my father's Indian Head nickels, enough for phone calls twice a week until we were both eighteen.

"It's too heavy," he said.

"It'll get lighter if you keep your promise," I said.

When he took off a little while later, I cried for three days. Then he called at our specified safe time to say he got picked up by a trucker hauling freight to the Delta, a man named Clemson Hynes.

"Thank God he wasn't an assfucker," Tommy laughed into the phone. "He's a good old guy."

Turns out, those were good years for him. Clemson took him all the way to Louisiana, to his own folks and his wife, who figured Tommy Bones was okay with them. He didn't get much school, but he learned crawfishing from Paw-Paw Hynes, and shrimping, and once in a while, he'd hop in with Clemson to share a run, taking the wheel so Clemson could climb into the cab and sleep.

Whenever he was free, Tommy hung around the dirtroad clubs, listening to Delta blues. He wrote me misspelled letters about the likes of Little Johnnie Brown and Sweet Mama Delmont. That's when he picked up the mouth harp, learning whatever he could after hours or before the clubs would open, when the musicians kicked back, having their free plates of dirty rice and pork. Finally, he was playing in the clubs himself, up on stage with Daddy Joe Crawley. I was just out of high school then, and studying photography. He was calling himself T-Bones, which somebody shortened to T-Bone, so eventually he was calling himself T-Bone Hynes, in honor of the people who gave him his only real home.

Over five years, we never lost touch, me always waiting for the time we'd settle in together, which we were supposed to do as soon as I moved off campus with my first real job. But that's when I first knew something wasn't right; because, when the time came, Tommy kept touring with his music, stopping in for only a week here and there, leaving in a hurry every time he found himself kissing or touching me too much.

"This has to stop," he'd always say.

"Why? Why can't you just treat me like any other girl?" He'd had his fair share already, and never made any secret of it.

"Because you'll never be like other girls to me," he said, "I don't want you to be."

"But I don't want to be set apart."

"There's no choice involved in that," he said. "It's just where you have to be for me." And then he'd be gone, sometimes for months, calling or sending letters as if there was nothing odd about what never happened between us.

This frustrating craziness had everything to do with my engagement to Kevin Joe. I figured Tommy would charge down the aisle at the last minute and rescue me from myself. But he didn't. He just stayed away an extra six months, then rented a house two blocks away from where Kevin and I lived. We started coordinating his touring around my freelance work, so that we could be together every minute it was possible, since that was about as much rescue as he was capable of.

"We've come a long way back," T-Bone said, "that sure as hell must mean something." The air of the shelter glowed like the inside of a bug light.

We didn't talk again until we finished off one of the quarts of beer, passing it back and forth between us. Then Tommy quietly unrolled our sleeping bags, doubling their size by zipping them together, and looking earnestly at me as he did.

"I figure this should be just like old times," he said.

"I know what you're trying to say," I told him.

He was still pretending June didn't happen. He wanted it to be like all those nights I snuck down there with him, when we lay side by side like angels, legs and arms entwined, but innocent. He was making it clear that when the lights were off, the two of us should nestle together beneath the down-filling, without the threat of passion. In the past I could see this as the purity of adoration, even when I throbbed between my legs and felt like death. But it was worse now that he let his guard down that one time and I believed everything between us could come true. Still, he kept sitting there on the sleeping bags, looking at me with those sad boy eyes which I always just hated to see.

"You know I try to understand," I sighed, crawling under the covers.

"That's all I ask," he answered, reaching up to extinguish the light.

I woke after a long sleep to total darkness. When I remembered where I was, I reached for the switch. But, as I stretched my arm toward the wall, Tommy stopped my hand.

"Let's keep it this way," he said.

"Completely dark?"

"Why not?" he said.

I couldn't think of a reason. I could never think my own thoughts too well when what Tommy wanted was strong. So, we stayed that way until we fell asleep again, talking for hours on our sleeping bags, each feeling, but not seeing the presence of the other. We felt our way to the flusher in blindness.

"I packed air freshener," T-Bone said. "So use it."

We ate in the dark, guessing what the food could be by holding it in our mouths and imagining.

"I think these are cheese curls," I said.

"And if this ain't trail mix, I'm eatin' bugs," he answered.

We stayed down there in blackness, and days must have gone by. Even though we talked less and less, I felt suspended and easeful, sometimes nearly blissful, moving through many cycles of sleeping and waking. But I worried what Tommy felt. Sometimes I sensed in the dark that he thought about death, and suspected that was what he meant for us—that he dreamed of solving things by letting us die—like reversing time and making it so we never were. It's not what I had in mind. After a day-long silence, I called his name.

"Tommy," I said, feeling his face turn toward me. "What if I'm naked?" I hugged my pile of discarded clothes against the softness of my belly.

"What if I am, too?" he said. "Would you be surprised?"

We slid beneath the covers quickly, locking together, flesh to flesh.

"Isn't there something about this, Midget, that feels like its righter than anywhere?"

"Haven't I been telling you that?" I said. He made me feel crazy.

Our bodies clung together like magnet shapes. I always knew they could. But now, with him admitting it, I was able to risk more than ever before, just to see.

"I could have a baby in me, Tommy."

In the silence his breath felt like a tide. And I don't think my heart was beating right.

"How long?" he finally said, meaning, I knew, could it be from the June night he pretended to forget.

"You would be the father," I said, easing the idea on him, feeling sure, if there was a baby, that he could be. "I'm pretty sure."

His bulk moved fast to pull away from me. A rush of cold against my body told me where he no longer lay.

"You can't do that," he said.

"I can too," I whispered, lying very still.

"It'll have to be Kevin Joe's."

"You know damn well it could never be Kev's."

"Don't do this, damn it," he said. "I never even wanted to be born myself, you know that. You can't bring something else of me to this world."

"It would be something of us, T-Bone," I reminded him. "You're just scared and you know it."

"You do this and you're stupid," he said. "I'll be gone."

"No, you won't. You've been with me my whole life Tommy Bones, in one way or another."

"Not anymore. You'd be by yourself with that faggot Kevin."

"Don't call him a faggot," I snapped, surprising myself.

"He IS a faggot," he said, angry at me now. "And I could beat shit out of him."

"Doesn't prove he's a faggot. Proves you're an ape."

"You see why we shouldn't talk?" he yelled. "This is just why."

I was sorry to have defended Kevin Joe, and tried to reach toward Tommy in the dark.

"Why would you make the kid a bastard?" he asked, pulling farther away. "When you know how it was for me?"

"Our child would never be a bastard," I said, still turning this way and that, trying to feel through the blackness for his form. I waited a long time, then whispered his name. He wouldn't answer. So, I curled up in a ball on my half of the sleeping bag, trying to feel him in the atmosphere around me, trying to let myself be rocked by the flow of his breathing.

Tomorrow, I thought, I'll try to get away. But even the word tomorrow held less meaning, since I couldn't tell when the edge of a new day might appear. And, anyway, there was something like safety here, for now, even in the darkest of places, so long as Tommy was willing to stay.

I was undecided about what to do as I drifted toward sleep. I might have slept for minutes or hours, I could have been dreaming, I don't know; but sometime later Tommy moved back beside me.

"Midget?" he whispered.

"Yeah?" I said, reaching out to touch his curly hair. It felt like lamb's wool in my fingers.

"This baby," he said. "Would you let me name it?"

"I could do that," I said, squeezing my eyelids tight, trying to make my senses buzz.

"Don't take this like me saying yes to something," he said. "But I'd name our kid Harley Davidson Hynes."

I felt like my whole body lifted, just a little, off the ground. Even when I snuggled my flesh against him and felt his clothes against my skin, I took it as a good sign that he didn't pull away.

"That's stupid," I said.

"I know."

"Okay then," I said, "Harley it is." A grin was splitting my face and I could barely stop myself from laughing out loud.

"Midge?" his voice came out from the darkness, "I'd still rather it not be real."

"That's okay," I said. It didn't have to be real now, just so long as I knew that he'd let it be. I could relax, in fact, because it didn't have to be.

"Isn't it better," T-Bone asked, "if this baby's just an idea between us?"

"Sure," I said, because that's what always felt best: All possibilities, just ideas between us. My body still felt like it was floating, my brain buzzing with happiness; I still grinned through the blackness, wide as my face could let my lips go.

Tommy's body relaxed against mine. Things were back to normal. And for a little while, everything stood still as it felt so damn right that I'd be smiling then and there, in the direction of a man who couldn't see me, that I'd be gulping down a laugh as big as the moon, just like a fool in the dark.

Night on Mt. Meru

. . . before dawn
His glory and his monuments are gone.
"Meru," W. B. Yeats

JUST BEFORE SUMMER'S END, Devlin left New Orleans. At the terminal, he held me to him and I could smell the spice of his cologne, feel the softness of his beard on my cheek.

"Are you going to be okay?" he whispered.

Too many people were moving around us, bumping and jostling to board the plane. They swirled like a mad river as Devlin drew me close. I had a hard time in his arms with so many eyes on us that way. How could people know I was his wife? And, maybe, what did they care? He had children near my age.

I nodded my answer to his question and held my expression in what I hoped was a typical way. I waved as he disappeared down the ramp, boarding a flight to Chicago. I stood watching as the plane taxied toward a runway. Only then, when I could see nothing more, did I walk alone through the airport, to hail the taxi which took me to my new apartment, the one Devlin knew nothing about.

I'd gotten my M.F.A. the spring before, but Devlin insisted I'd do better with a Ph.D. in Art History. I applied to make him happy, but never expected that they'd accept me. Devlin swore he didn't pull any strings, and urged me to begin the study. I decided my area of specialty would be the Hindu Art of the Khmer, which I studied because my father went MIA, as far as we could discover, around Dac Lap, near the Cambodian border, in 1968, six years before.

My mother never believed a thing the Army said, and she certainly wasn't about to believe that my father was really missing, any more than she believed when they eventually declared him dead.

"Your father's a Green Beret," she said, swearing to my sister and me that it was all a pretense. "He's gone underground is all," she said. "You'll see."

So the three of us lived in a dream, each in our own way. My sister raised the flag on our flagpole each morning, believing somehow that daddy could see it, wherever he was, and that, like a beacon from a lighthouse, it would guide him home from any jungle cave. My mother watched the news ferociously, perched like a blackbird on the edge of her old blue armchair in the livingroom. Each time a mention of Cambodian activities was made, she'd lean forward more eagerly, nodding to herself. It was as if every incursion into Cambodian territory, every internal political struggle in Phnom Penh had Roy Meade behind it. And me? I escaped early to college, and made art.

I was just seventeen then, and ill-prepared for the civilian world. Nearly all my life, I'd lived on post at Fort Bragg, where the military presence was all there is. I breathed in the regimentation that permeated the air. I expected all men to be in camouflage. And while all the rest of America was carrying banners protesting the war, Fort Bragg was sending boys off with great ceremony and fervor into battle. Whether I believed in the war or not was never questioned. There simply *was* a war in the world of Bragg and my family, my life, my being were bound to it.

There at school I rarely spoke of myself or my family, or my father's involvement in the war—not to the other students and not even to most of my professors, who were themselves very young, and who frequently led discussions in class about draft evasion, or civil disobedience. I had a secret life that would have been despised here. So I submerged myself in the Fine Arts program, swam in the tides of creativity, breathed air filled with paint fumes, kneaded clay.

I felt very alone until I entered a class called "Myth and History: The Confluence of Art and Memory." The man who entered and stood at the podium was older, but WASP-ishly elegant, tanned, devastatingly handsome. Dr. Devlin MacVeigh, newly appointed as Chair of the Classics Department, was full of enthusiasm and passion for his subject and his students. I loved watching him teach. He would move quickly across the classroom, writing on the board, challenging students to dig into themselves for deeper understandings of mythic meaning.

"There is a collective memory," he said. "A place where all knowledge is stored, all images shared. Is it truth? Or 'manifold illusion'?"

I wondered: who wanted to find that place he so believed in, where memory is stored, where images are understood? It had to be truth, I thought. Truth had to live somewhere. But why would we search for it? Something in me was afraid of truth.

Still, it was in that class, and under his tutelage, that I began my earliest study of Hindu mythology.

Sitting in his office during conference time, I presented my idea: a comparative study between the symbolism of Mt. Meru, the Hindu mountain where the gods dwell, and Mt. Olympus, the mountain home of the Greek gods.

He leaned back in his chair, holding a mug of coffee in his hands. There was a small smile on his face and his blue eyes were lit by the sunlight coming through his window.

"Why Hindu mythology?" he asked.

"Because I want to study Cambodia," I said. "To understand the Hinduism of Angkor."

He sat very still, and a look of seriousness crossed his face. "Why Cambodia?" he asked quietly.

And I found myself telling him: my mother's determined belief, my imaginings of my father.

"It's a very dangerous place now," he said.

I nodded. "But I look at the pictures and Angkor is so beautiful, so fierce. I like to think that he is there."

Devlin had put his cup down and moved his chair closer to mine. He leaned forward, his hand on his beard, his eyes trained sharply on my face.

"I think, if he's there, and if I study it, we'll stay connected," I said, trying not to cry.

"Like magic?" he asked, handing me a tissue.

"Some kind of magic," I admitted.

"To bring him back?"

"Call him back, maybe. Like a sound that he could follow."

He told me that he would approve the study.

"It's an important area of research," he said. "Besides, it gives you hope."

"No," I said. "It keeps me angry."

He frowned.

"If he's there," I said, "and if he wants to be there, that means he doesn't want to be with us."

Devlin put his hands over mine. It was the first time he touched me, and a very brave thing to do. Or crazy. He told me later that it astonished him, terrified him.

"There is always anger," he said.

I shook my head at him, liking the way my hand felt inside his. "I don't think you could know," I said. "You live in this world I never even knew about," I looked around his mahogany office, "with your Greek books and Caesar's Gaelic Wars . . ."

A look on his face stopped me from talking. We stared at each other a few seconds before he spoke.

"My youngest son died last year," he said, "near Khe Sanh."

So now, at Devlin's urging, I'm set to study everything I can about Cambodia. I won't be able to avoid thinking of my father, imagining him living off the land in the jungles around Angkor Wat, or holding court with the macaques who wander the abandoned palaces and temples of that ancient citadel. I'll envision him gathering tribes of the Khmer Serei around him in preparation for the heroic triumph against the forces of darkness my mother insisted he would achieve.

Was I doing this work for my father? For Devlin? I don't know. I wasn't doing it for myself. At least I don't think I was.

It's over five years ago now since we met, and I have been happy with Devlin. I love him. But when he told me that he had been invited as visiting professor to spend a semester at the University of Chicago, I knew I would have to leave if he accepted. I didn't tell him.

It had been a crazy summer. Watergate used up everybody's energy. Devlin spent the months watching the hearings, as I painted. I'd been offered a small show at a gallery on Decatur Street. Everything was a blur of July heat, endless TV coverage, acrylics and oils, brushes and palette knives, and paint stains on my spaghetti-strap t-shirts.

And then came this invitation to Chicago. When Devlin told me that he'd accepted, I said nothing. I quietly signed the lease to the third floor walkup off Jackson Square and secretly began to pack boxes.

Fall classes began and everyone had gone dead, or into shock. The Art History Department had me teaching two intro courses as well as carrying a full-time load of graduate courses. I was sleepwalking mostly, which was not a good way to start. I called Devlin each night from the new apartment, never letting on that anything had changed. I talked about my classes and my students. He talked about his work in Chicago, the visiting faculty appointment, the anthology collaboration that was part of the semester's activities. I always meant to tell him that I had moved away. But when the opportunities came, the words froze in my throat. I told myself that he already knew, that he must know, that he knew me too well to think I could bear that big home, sitting empty, after he left. I'm afraid of big houses, with their dark shadowy corners. They make me feel very small and alone.

I stayed by myself in my apartment both day and night, studying the vistas and rhythms of my transplanted life. I contemplated the hushed, tourmaline mornings, with the slide of my feet on hand-polished hardwood; I immersed myself in the warm, cream-colored afternoons with Earl Grey in Minton cups. As I unpacked my boxes, I found Miss Huggins, a favorite doll of my childhood, and gave her a place of honor leaning on the pillows of my loft bed, tucked up under the rafters. An old red and white bead necklace, which I still sometimes wore, reminded me of my five-year-old self. Sometimes it felt like it was working, that I'd found my way back to a place within me that was distant and still and pure. But in the endless nights, it all failed. I'd wake, sometimes thrashing against a dark weight crushing me, suffocating me. Imagining gunshots in the sounds of the revelers in the alley below, frightened by the low moans of the boats on the Mississippi, the spirits and ghosts of my life swirling in the air above my head, all of it combining to terrify me. So I'd hold Miss Huggins to my chest and whisper out loud to the dark that I was sorry, so sorry for all the bad inside me.

When Thanksgiving came, Devlin returned home for the holiday with no clue that I wouldn't be there waiting. I could have pretended, and just gone back as if I'd never left. But I couldn't return. He had left me, as I always knew he would.

I stayed where I was, hiding from him, from his assurances. Hiding from anything he might say that could coax me back into believing that he would keep me safe, that he would always stay. If I had to lose him sometime, it might as well be now.

Back at school the Monday after Thanksgiving break, I saw Devlin on campus moving through the crowd. I slipped quickly past the students gathered at the door of my building, and into the medieval pretense of my lobby. I moved across the worn Tabriz toward an open elevator. But Devlin had already seen me, and entered the elevator, too. We were not alone, so neither of us spoke until the doors opened on my department's floor, and he took me by the hand. He guided me without words into the lounge and closed the door.

"Rachael," he said. "I've been frantic. Where have you been?"

I didn't know how to explain myself. I expected, as I stood there unable to answer, that Devlin's voice would take a condescending tone, that he would treat me like the idiot child I felt I was. He didn't.

"I couldn't find you all weekend," he said, "I called the police. I called everyone. No one knew where you were."

Seeing the pain in his face, I felt my tears beginning to rise. Glancing out the door of the lounge, I saw people standing close by.

"Could we not talk now?" I said. "I don't want to cry here."

"There's no other time, Rachael. You owe me an explanation."

"I'm not living there anymore," I said. "I thought you knew."

He looked stricken and tired. "Well of course I know now," he said.

I knew that his face would look like that, what sadness there would be in his eyes. I hated myself; still, I said nothing.

Finally, Devlin spoke again. "Rachael, when did you leave?"

"You left, Devlin. You went first."

"I went to teach, Rachael. You said you understood."

"You wanted me to say it. So I said it."

"I asked you to tell me the truth. You know I didn't leave you. I love you."

"You won't come back," I said. "You walked out the door and flew away. Now you'll disappear. Or you'll die. And I won't be able to take it."

Devlin drew me to him, and I felt myself relax for the first time in months, wrapped there in his arms.

"I should have foreseen what this would cause," he said.

I began to cry. "You're going to leave me someday, Devlin, no matter what."

He leaned away from our embrace, still holding me. He shook his head, no, about to speak. I lifted my hand to his lips to stop him.

"One way or another," I said.

Devlin dropped his arms and stepped away from me. He looked intensely at me, then sat slowly on an ottoman, with his face in his hands.

We were both quiet.

Classes began changing, and the hallway outside filled with students. A few looked through the window in the door, about to enter, then moved away.

When Devlin spoke again, his voice was tired. "It's true what you say, Rachael," he said. "I will die, and quite likely much sooner than you."

I began to cry again.

Still sitting on the ottoman before me, he reached out for my hand. I reached back. "Can't we work through this?" he said.

I shook my head. "You always encouraged me to discover what I feel," I said. "And I feel that I need to run away."

He smiled sadly. "Why does the first feeling you act on have to be this one?"

I squeezed his hand, then let it go. "I'm sorry, Devlin," I said. "I have to stay away."

He nodded and stood up. "I'm not giving up," he said. "I'll be home before Christmas."

I nodded in reply but didn't say anything.

He kissed my forehead and quietly put his arms around me. "I wish you would let me in," he said.

"I don't know how," I whispered.

"You can start by telling me where you are living," Devlin said.

"Okay," I said.

"You disappear, Rachael. You. I'm still here."

After he left, I stood alone for a while, wrapping my own arms around myself, wondering if I would ever understand the eternal tumult inside me.

ONLY A SHORT TIME remained before the end of the term. I was working to finish all my own research and to write my own papers, all the while teaching and grading papers for my students. On one of the last days of the semester, the Art History floor was nearly empty, with evening approaching. Classes were over. Lights from the Chairman's office glowed into the shadows as I approached to drop off my grades. Nella, the Chairman, looked up at me.

"Faculty Christmas party tomorrow night," she smiled.

"Nella, I'm excusing myself from the party this year."

"No way," she said, quickly.

"Come on," I said, frowning at her. "I've done it to death."

"As Devlin's child lover. Now you'll come as Devlin's estranged wife."

I couldn't hide my surprise. "Do people know about the separation? I thought it was a secret."

Nella burst out laughing. "He was calling all over the city looking for you at Thanksgiving. And even without that, Rachael, you should know that in academia, nothing personal is ever a secret."

"People are talking?"

"Of course. Nixon resigned four months ago. We're desperate for new scandal."

"I don't want Devlin to be embarrassed," I said. "He doesn't deserve the scandal."

"Little one, for Devlin, marrying you was more scandalous than being separated. This makes him look sympathetic instead of crazy."

"Oh Nella, then I really can't go. People will think I'm horrible."

"Don't be ridiculous. You want tenure someday? Endure it."

Heading home, I rounded the corner onto Chartres, and felt a stir of chilled air rolling in from the river. The bells of the Cathedral chimed the lateness of the hour and I moved slowly, fighting an urge to look over my shoulder. Everyone knows there are ghosts here; and I know that I have some of my own following me. I pulled my scarf more securely around my neck and tucked my head low in the dampness, listening to how my boots tapped sharply against the cold bricks of the alleyway, first one step then another, until I reached my door. My apartment on Pirate's Alley had an exposed brick wall and window that opened to the alley beneath. The lights from the Café and Absinthe House below glowed softly throughout the night, sending a reddened glimmer through my windows that dimly lit my rooms, making it hard to recognize dawn.

AT THE CHRISTMAS PARTY, I downed three flutes of Moët on an empty stomach by the time Nella found me.

"I'm jealous," she said as she slid up to me. "It's been decades since I could risk a dress like that."

"I'm drunk," I said.

"Perfect," she laughed.

"I warned you," I mumbled.

"Oh hell," she laughed. "I live for these moments."

I expected that I would have trouble seeing Devlin. He'd be holding court at the center of the few remaining faculty members in the Classics Department. I worried that seeing him might crack this resistance I didn't understand. I drank more champagne.

What I never expected was the way my breath caught in my chest when I spotted one of my professors. Bastian Asura was nearby, posing against the furniture wearing a baggy linen suit and sandals. I was trying to pretend not to see him when he looked up at me and frowned. Nella leaned over and whispered, "He's the new one in Asian Studies. He's fascinating."

"I was in his seminar last semester," I said, frowning back in his direction.

I had been the last one to leave his classroom one evening, and he took me by the arm.

"Stay," he said, softly.

His dark pony-tailed hair was marbled with strands of grey. There was a fusion of stone tones in his eyes. He reminded me of the carved figures near Angkor's Elephant Gates, where the devata shows her teeth.

"Have a drink with me? We could discuss your paper," he said.

"I have to go," I said.

"What's the hurry?" he smiled.

He frightened me. I wasn't sure why.

"Rachael Meade-MacVeigh," he said. "A lady of mystery."

"Not mysterious at all," I said.

He shook his head. "I can tell when someone is hiding something. What is your secret?" He leaned in toward me. "I know that you have one."

I lifted my briefcase to my chest, feeling very uneasy inside. "I don't," I said. "I don't have any secrets."

I hurried away and was sure to be the first to leave his class for the rest of the semester.

"Look to his left," Nella said.

An aging waif of a woman stood by his side.

"She's a potter and a yoga instructor," Nella snorted.

"How do you know these things?" I asked, unable to take my eyes off the woman's creased face, frizzy braid and sun-browned skin. I knew that, on close inspection, her toes would be slightly dirty.

"Where did he find *her*?"

"Berkeley," Nella said. "Class of '65. Both of them. Where the hell else do you find people like that?"

"Berkeley, '65," I repeated.

I saw Nella's face, and knew that she knew.

"Holy Matilda," she said. "He didn't let on there was a wife."

"Stop," I whispered.

She smirked. "That's so fucking typical."

"Please," I said. "It was meaningless."

"Like hell," she said. "You're shaking. And he stares whenever you're not looking."

I was holding yet another champagne flute—hanging on, actually, with both hands. So I took a long drink and glowered in Asura's direction until he turned away. Then I said something to Nella about using the bathroom, and stumbled upstairs. Suddenly, I wanted to throw up. I skidded into the open bathroom and stood there, staring at the flush of my face in the mirror. I tried to believe it was all alcohol, because my stomach was clenched and my palms were sweaty. But there was a pain around my heart that alcohol didn't explain. Asura saw something—a secret he said. I tried to calm myself. You're being silly, I whispered to the mirror. As I began to powder the shine away from my nose, Bastian appeared in the hall and entered. He closed the bathroom door behind him, locked it and crossed his arms.

"You're pissy as ever," he smiled.

"Please get out of here," I said.

"Be nice, Rachael," he smiled. "I could always lower your grade."

"I'm not feeling well. I'm going to throw up," I choked.

"Oh, I'm staying for that," he said.

I turned my back to him, trying to steady myself. What was frightening me so much?

"Come here," he said. He pulled a washcloth off the towel rack and ran it under cold water. He drew me closer and held the cool cloth against my forehead, my checks, my neck. "Better?" he said.

I nodded.

"Come closer," he grinned. "I want to touch this dress you're almost wearing."

I pulled away from him. "My husband is downstairs," I said.

"Estranged, I hear," Asura answered. "Doesn't count."

"And you have a wife," I said.

He watched me for a moment. "Judith is nothing like she was when I married her."

"Oh come ON," I said. "That woman hasn't changed a thing since the Johnson Administration."

He shrugged. "Maybe I'VE changed."

"Please leave me alone."

Instead, he took my face in his hands and kissed me.

"Just go away," I said, but I couldn't move. I had turned to stone.

A smile spread across his face. When he kissed me again, I kissed him back. I didn't mean to. But by the time he left, his hands had found their way all over my body, and I had collapsed against the wall, heart thumping, body shaking, betrayed by my lack of self-protective powers.

I pulled myself to standing and redid my face. Concentrating as I lined my eyes and smudged the shadow, I was able to calm my breathing and prepare to enter the party downstairs. By the time I had powdered, I could almost hope to convince myself that nothing had happened. There was a grey and smoky place inside me where things like this hid, I suspected.

I searched for Devlin as I returned to the livingroom and was shocked, when I found him, to see a strange woman glance at me, then quickly put her hand protectively on his arm. He looked surprisingly well, too, even better than I'd expected; and I began to realize that he hadn't asked me to come home in any of our recent conversations. I marched directly toward him and stopped sharply in front of the woman.

"Excuse me," I said. "I'd like to speak to my husband."

The woman looked at Devlin without moving.

"Virginia," he smiled. "I'll be just fine."

"Who are you, Virginia?" I asked.

"Rachael," Devlin warned.

"Who is she, Devlin? Some kind of geriatric bodyguard?"

"I'm only fifty-two," she said, her hand at her throat.

"Then life's been hard on you," I said. "Now PLEASE get the hell out of here."

After she walked away, Devlin turned to me with an angry frown. "Really, Rachael, that's the worst public display I've seen in quite some time."

"She had her hands all over you," I said.

"Rachael," Devlin began.

"I'm not jealous," I interrupted, "so don't look smug."

"Come home," he said. "Have you been drinking?"

"Did you bring her?"

"Of course not," he said. "Come home. Whatever is happening with you, we should face it together. For the sake of this relationship."

"There's no relationship, Devlin." I was so angry with him. "I left you."

Devlin shook his head. "There is always a relationship, Rachael. It doesn't disappear."

"I don't want to talk about this."

"Then why did you come over here?" he asked.

"Because that old moose had her arm around you," I said.

"Rachael," he said, taking my hand. "She touched my arm."

"You shouldn't be letting people touch you like that," I said.

Devlin steered me into a quiet corner. "Rachael, you've left everything in your studio. The gallery director called, asking how the work was going."

"I'll finish it," I snapped.

"Do you mean to postpone?"

"I don't know," I said.

"You've left your work behind, Rachael. You must mean to come back."

"You'd like to think that, Devlin," I said. "But it's not true."

Devlin stared at me. "Are you sure?"

I wasn't. "Yes," I said. "I actually bought china. It's Minton."

Devlin watched me quietly for a minute. "This threatens to do horrible things to us," he said. "Is that what you want?"

"No," I said. "I'm scared." I hadn't meant to say that.

"Then don't do this," he said.

"I have to go," I said, moving away.

"Rachael," Devlin said, then stopped.

I waited, watching him struggle with himself. He looked sadly into my face, then off into another corner of the room.

"Asura," he said, closing his eyes for a moment. "Asura is a despicable human being."

I DON'T REMEMBER leaving the party. I think Nella brought me home. The next morning, when the banging began at my door, I had no idea what time of day or night it was. I climbed quickly from the loft to answer, fearing that it was something to do with Devlin, some emergency. Instead, it was Asura, holding a box of English Breakfast Tea and a bag of beignets. The clock showed that it was barely dawn.

"Get out of here," I said, trying to close the door. "Go ahead and fail me if you want. Just go."

He moved to block me. "Please," he said softly. "I'm making a fool of myself. Can't you see that?"

I stopped.

He looked earnestly at me. "Please," he said again.

"It's 6 a.m.," I said. "You don't belong here."

"I've been up all night, walking," he said. "I had to see you."

I hesitated.

"Just a cup of tea," he said. "And then I'll leave."

I let him in. Just as I was closing my door, my only neighbor on the third floor, an emergency room night nurse named Beverly, opened her door. She was still dressed in her uniform, with small spatters of blood on the bodice.

"Is everything okay, Rachael?" she asked.

I nodded. "I think so."

Her glance took in everything: my skimpy t-shirt and pajama pants, Asura standing beside me now. She frowned.

"Just yell if you need me," she said.

I nodded again. "Get some rest," I said. "Looks like it was a rough night."

She was still frowning. "Okay," she said, closing her door.

"That bitch needs to mind her own business," Asura said.

I looked at him sharply. "How did you get this address?" I asked.

He smiled. "Easy. I bribed the secretary of your department last week."

I had been walking into the living room. I stopped. "Last week?" I repeated.

He shrugged. "I've been watching you for months, Rachael. There's something about you I have to know more about." He walked toward my kitchen. "Where are your cups?"

I followed behind him and boiled the water; I set out the tea set. In the livingroom, I sat where he told me to and let him pour out the tea. He was in total control. That little vulnerable boy at the door had disappeared. I didn't know if he really had been up all night. But he was wide awake and dressed. I still wore only my T-shirt and pajama pants. When he sat beside me on the couch, he began to play with my hair. I was beginning to feel dazed.

"Do you remember *Twelfth Night*?" he asked.

I nodded.

"My mother was British," he said. "She loved Shakespeare. She chose the name Sebastian before I was born, hoping my arrival would clear things up—like the play."

He stopped talking just long enough to give me a very slow, very thorough kiss on the neck. I allowed the kiss without protest. He moved his hand through my hair again.

"Except in this case, I was supposed to clear up the marriage."

I sat very still. My heart felt funny in my chest again.

Bastian stared into his teacup for a few minutes. "But my father returned to Tokyo before she and I came home from the hospital. He took his mistress with him." He looked quietly at me for a few moments. "He never laid eyes on me," he said.

I didn't know what to say. We sat silently for a while.

When Bastian spoke again, he took my hand. "Today is my birthday, Rachael. I had to spend it with someone who would understand."

"I don't understand anything," I said.

He kissed me again, this time on the mouth. "That's okay," he whispered. "It's probably not my birthday, anyway."

He had my panties off before the tea was cold. By the second time we'd had sex, I knew I didn't even like him. I was in some kind of terrible trouble, and had no control over what was going on. I felt anesthetized, outside of myself, not even there enough to know what to do.

By that night, we'd had sex so many times that my body was raw.

"I can't even go to the bathroom," I said, stumbling back through the kitchen.

"You'll be fine," he said. "You'll be ready for me to come back before you know it."

"No," I said. "You can't come back."

He laughed softly, running his fingers softly up my thigh.

"Of course I can," he said.

I just stared at him.

"You should make me a key," he said.

I shook my head no. He took his hand to my chin and moved my head up and down.

"That's a good girl," he said. "I am going to need one."

For hours after Bastian left, I stayed curled on the sofa, letting the lights and sounds of The Quarter wash over me. It was the second time since meeting Devlin all those years ago that I felt so lost, so worthless. I wanted my husband. I did. I wanted to talk to him. I wanted, maybe, actually, to go home. But I didn't deserve to go home anymore. Not after this. I hadn't ever deserved Devlin to begin with. I felt like someone struggling to wake up from anesthesia, or fighting a kind of amnesia that grips you tight, that pulls you back inside a forgetfulness so black that there is no hope of knowing yourself.

THE NEXT DAY was Monday, and I didn't teach until afternoon. I knew the only way I could recover some sanity was to go to Devlin's house. I could check on my studio, work on some of my canvases, settle my nerves. It hurt me to think I hadn't painted since late summer, and I didn't understand why I wasn't able to work.

I rode the streetcar, and then walked down Prytania, stopping a moment to stare up at the second floor windows before opening the gate. I stared through the leaded glass, but could see only shadow. Maybe Devlin was up there already, working in his study. Maybe he was standing there, with his second cup of coffee, watching down at me. Maybe he'd come and tell me, once again, to come home. And, since I was already there, maybe I could actually just manage to stay. Or, I thought, maybe Virginia spent the night and they were both up there at that very moment trying to figure out how to avoid me.

"Aw, the hell with it," I said out loud, wiping damp palms on the thighs of my jeans, then lifting the latch to enter. If he was up there, he wouldn't come down. Why should he? After the Christmas party, he had every right to be angry. If I wanted to see him, it was up to me. I'd have to go up to the house myself, make amends, and I knew I couldn't do that. I wasn't ready. I was ashamed.

Loose stones kicked up around my feet as I walked around the side of the house and headed toward the carriage house that had served as my studio since our marriage.

Inside the carriage house, the meringue glow of morning half-lit the unfinished canvases scattered through the studio. A desk piled high with sketchbooks stood in the corner. The smell of linseed oil permeated the atmosphere, quickly entering my nostrils and throat. I had no idea what drove me to leave here, to stay away so long.

"What am I doing?" I muttered to myself.

Sounds echoed back to me, floated around me in the shadows and the light.

I don't think I ever really intended to take my paintings away in the first place. Devlin was right. They belonged where they were, in the sweet air of this genteel structure, surrounded with its flower gardens and whispering trees. They were born there, and I'd half expected, as I looked at the canvases, to find that they had finished themselves in my absence, so much of a life did I feel in them. But they had waited, expectant, containing all the potential that was meant to flow to them through me. I had to be brave enough to open myself so that they could find completion.

I looked at the half-finished work. The images frightened me. What had escaped from inside me that now lived on these canvases? On one, a crocodile peered from beneath a tangle of red roses, a little brown man raising a hammer in the shadows. In another, a little girl in makeup danced on the fingers of a large hand. In a third, a man on fire lit the air around three girls, standing on the banks of a raging Mississippi River. In the catalogue prepared by the gallery owner, she calls this work "surreal," or says they are "dreamscapes." I don't correct her.

"I can't go farther," I whispered to the images. "Don't you understand?"

The air was still. I felt chastised by their silence, by their refusal to allow me to refuse.

I lifted a handful of brushes and held them like a bride's bouquet, wishing I knew how to pray.

"I can't do it!" I cried, hurling the brushes at the wall. "I won't!"

Asura came again and again; there seemed to be no use in telling him to leave me alone. He did what he wanted, and I let him. And what he wanted were secret trysts and sexual perversions I will not detail, although I allowed, and remained partially present, through every sort of act. A dim voice worried inside myself: Is this who I've always been?

At first I played with the idea that it was some kind of crazy passion, but that was a lie, and I nearly always knew it. Something closer to pure hatred is what brought him there, and some part of me wanted to be hated. That's all I've been able to see so far. And that there's an arousal born from pain more powerful, almost, than love.

Spring semester began, and I dressed carefully to conceal the bruises. Nella saw me in the mail room.

"You're awfully quiet these days," she said. "What's going on?"

Before I was ready to respond, she fixed me with a stare. "Something's creepy," she said, plucking a cigarette from her purse and lighting it.

I shrugged, watching the small flame, trying to look nonchalant.

"You know, I suppose, he's the kind of guy who sets fire to women, then stands back and lets them burn," she said, shaking out her match.

Something caught in my throat. "What?" I said. "Who?"

She raised her eyebrows at me. I felt heat rushing to my cheeks.

"Does the entire faculty know about this too?" I asked.

She took a long drag of her cigarette, keeping her eyes on my face. Sighing her exhale, she glanced out the window.

"You owed it to Devlin to tell him yourself, you know. It was the least you could have done."

"He knew before I did, Nella."

Her face took on a rocky sternness. "What you thought he knew is irrelevant. The point is, he deserves better."

"I know," I said. "It's been so long since I knew where I was going, Nella. I don't know myself. I don't know how Asura is doing this to me."

"What exactly is he doing?" Her face had softened a little. "Are you okay?"

"No," I admitted. "I'm not." I paused. "He hurts me, Nella. Physically."

She stared at me. "You *allow* this?"

I nodded, ashamed.

"Do you want to call my therapist?"

"No," I said. "I'm afraid of therapists."

She wrote a number and handed it to me. "Then call this."

It was Devlin's number.

"I have no right to do that anymore."

"Rachael, that man could have anyone he wants. You and I both know that. But he's out there, even now, willing to be your Constant North. And you're so god-damned young, you don't even know what that's worth."

I HAD BEGUN WALKING The Quarter every day, past the places of my childhood. Exchange Alley. Esplanade, at the edge of Marigny. The courtyard of my great-aunt's home which stood cold and empty since her death. I was staying up all night, afraid to fall asleep because of the fragments of feelings and memories flying through my mind, through the shadows when darkness fell. I kept the red and white beads near my pillow, and pulled Miss Huggins close. I sat until the sun came up, reading through notebooks I had written in since childhood and yet, somehow, had never opened before.

The news on the TV was filled with accounts of the last gasps of struggle in South Vietnam. The North Vietnamese had rolled through Da Nang and Tam Ky with no resistance. They were heading for Chu Lai. Despite the military funeral the Army gave, my mother still wrote me to say that her husband, my father, was out there somewhere—maybe still in or around Saigon, maybe deep in the jungles where the insertions were never admitted to. Some part of me believed it too. Wanted to believe. But why?

One afternoon in late April, I walked into my apartment to find Bastian waiting there, his back toward the door. He had left several notes in my mailbox on campus, insisting that we meet. He held me without saying a word. Then, looking at me for a moment, he began to unbutton my blouse.

"Judith has given me an ultimatum," he said, slipping the blouse off my shoulders. "She says never to see you again."

"Stop it," I said, pulling my shirt out of his hands. "Are you going to leave her?"

"I never leave," he said calmly. "She always knows, and I never leave."

He watched me as I gathered my blouse back around me.

He tried to kiss me. I held my lips closed against him, and turned my face away. He took my face in his hands and squeezed my cheeks together, making a face at me.

"No tears?" he said, smiling. "I have never been able to make you cry. Even when I've actually drawn blood." He slid his hand right down into my panties, and I couldn't even stop him. He stroked me hard until I came; then he let me go and walked out the door.

I LAY IN BED all that afternoon and into the night, wide awake, feeling sick to my stomach, shivering and crying. Could these thoughts be memories? Could the images that visited my dreams be true?

Hours went by but I never fell asleep. Then, when the clock hit 3 a.m., the lock clicked and light fell across the floor as he walked back into the apartment. I lay very still and didn't say a word.

"I have actually sobbed," he said. "I'm desolate."

"Get out of here," I whispered. My voice was weak, but it was there. Beginning to be there.

"Judith never gives me ultimatums, Rachael," he said. "I lied."

I waited, silent in the darkness.

"Take me back, Rachael."

"Go away," I said, a little louder. "You've won. I am destroyed."

"That's not how I win," he said. "I win when you take me back anyway. Don't you know this game?"

His form cast a long shadow across the carpet. The light of the bar downstairs glowed red through the window, lighting his frame. He flipped my housekey onto the table in the darkness.

"We'll see how long it takes you," he said.

He moved toward the door slowly, in case I wanted to stop him. When I didn't call to him, his voice came from the darkness below.

"I know the secret. You're always afraid, aren't you? And now, you think because you've allowed this that you must be a monster like me. You're not. You could never be. Someone like you is just destined for a downfall. I knew how to make it happen. You couldn't possibly have stopped it."

"Get out, Bastian. For God's sake," I said.

He did. And I lay on the bed, staring up into the darkness, listening to his footsteps on the three flights of stairs growing more distant as they approached the street door. Tears slid out the sides of my eyes and into the curves of my ears, and I heard the huge door open below me, then slam. An enormous wave broke over me, washing some part of me away. *Not a monster.* He said. *I am not a monster.* I was sobbing now like a little girl, holding Miss Huggins, remembering things I couldn't bear.

THE DESIRE CAME SUDDENLY; then, just as suddenly I was moving through the front gate, unlocking his front door. I needed Devlin. The house was dark as I entered, and I moved slowly through the foyer and up the staircase. In the hall, a sconce glowed on the wall, lighting the entrance of Devlin's room.

"Devlin?" I whispered, slowly moving into the room, allowing my eyes to adjust in the darkness.

He wasn't there. It was 4 a.m. I moved toward his wing chair by the window and sat, leaning my body into its firmness. I wanted to be enveloped by the chair's shape and solidity. Sitting there I felt safer than I had in days. I didn't think, didn't count the time, didn't worry about what would happen next. Even as the small light in the foyer downstairs clicked on and eased a glow gently into the edges of the room, I sat, not willing to move from this space.

"Rachael?" Devlin whispered. "Are you here?"

"In your room," I answered.

There was a hesitation, then he climbed the stairs and entered.

"Are you all right?"

I nodded, still curled tight, feeling even more like a child. "Is Virginia here? Because I couldn't stand it if she were here."

He shook his head. "Of course not. I guess I fell asleep in the study, watching the news. I was with Reynolds earlier. Budget struggles."

"Enrollment down?"

"Rachael, I run the Classics Department. Enrollment is always down. What are you doing here?"

"I was afraid."

"I know. It's horrifying, all of this."

"You know?"

Devlin hesitated, watching me. "Of course I do. It's all over the news."

I looked at him without comprehending. He took my hand, studying my face closely.

"Saigon," he said. "It's fallen. Vietnam is lost."

"Saigon?" I repeated. The word moved through my mind, from the back to the front, like one more dream I could barely remember.

He sat down on the bed, still looking closely at me. I turned my head away, pressing my face against the back of the chair. I closed my eyes, trying to take in what he just told me, trying to will it to be untrue. I thought, *Saigon*. I thought, *My father*.

Devlin rose and pulled the comforter down, turning the sheet aside and plumping the pillows. When he turned toward me, I was afraid of what he might say. But I needn't have worried.

"You sleep here," he said. "I'll take the bed in the guest-room. Tomorrow we'll start sorting this mess out."

I stood, sliding out of my jeans and climbing into bed. Devlin smoothed the blankets around me and kissed my forehead.

"I didn't leave you, Rachael," he whispered. "I wish you could understand that."

But I hadn't understood. There is still so much I don't understand. More than ever before.

Devlin sighed. "About Asura?" he asked.

"I thought," I said, staring into his eyes.

"That it was love?" he said hoarsely.

He was afraid to hear my answer. I could feel that in the air between us.

"No," I said. I knew it wasn't that. I almost always knew it wasn't that.

His body relaxed. "Then we'll survive this, if you want us to," he said.

Part of me wanted to believe that could be true. Another part was already slipping out of reach. I gripped the blankets on my husband's bed, hoping to hang on.

"Devlin," I said.

"I know," he answered. "Honey, I know."

"I'm sliding," I told him. "I'm losing hold."

He took my hand. "Then take me with you this time," he said. "Let me see where you go."

"Keep me here," I insisted, and gripped his hand tighter. "Keep me safe."

Devlin wrapped his arms around me, rocking me gently. "I will always try," he said.

Defeat was at a distant gate. Smoke rose over ruined horizons, the desolation of reality. Still, the light of the pre-dawn air between us was sweet with promise, and no one noticed, and no one said, if I had asked too much.

www.ingramcontent.com/pod-product-compliance
Lightning Source LLC
Chambersburg PA
CBHW032147020726
47496CB00003B/748